· A QUINNIE BOYD MYSTERY ·

VAMPIRES ON THE RUN

C. M. SURRISI

Carolrhoda Books • Minneapolis

Carolrhoda Books
A division of Lerner Publishing Group, Inc.
241 First Avenue North
Minneapolis, MN 55401 USA

For reading levels and more information, look up this title at www.lernerbooks.com.

Jacket illustration by Elizabeth Baddeley.
Map design by Ingrid Sundberg.
Backgrounds interior: © Gordan/Bigstock.com.

Main body text set in Bembo Std 12.5/17. Typeface provided by Monotype.


**Library of Congress Cataloging-in-Publication Data**

Names: Surrisi, Cynthia, author.
Title: Vampires on the run : a Quinnie Boyd mystery / C.M. Surrisi.
Description: Minneapolis : Carolrhoda Books, [2017] | Summary: "Two suspicious writers from New York arrive in Quinnie Boyd's small Maine town. They claim to be the confidants of a vampire count. But Quinnie begins to wonder if the authors are vampires themselves" —Provided by publisher.
Identifiers: LCCN 2016016920 (print) | LCCN 2016034208 (ebook) | ISBN 9781512411508 (th : alk. paper) | ISBN 9781512426922 (eb pdf)
Subjects: | CYAC: Mystery and detective stories. | Vampires—Fiction. | Friendship—Fiction. | Maine—Fiction.
Classification: LCC PZ7.1.S88 Vam 2017 (print) | LCC PZ7.1.S88 (ebook) | DDC [Fic]—dc23

LC record available at https://lccn.loc.gov/2016016920

Manufactured in the United States of America
1-39659-21288-5/24/2016

For my brilliant, brave, and
sweet-hearted Magda

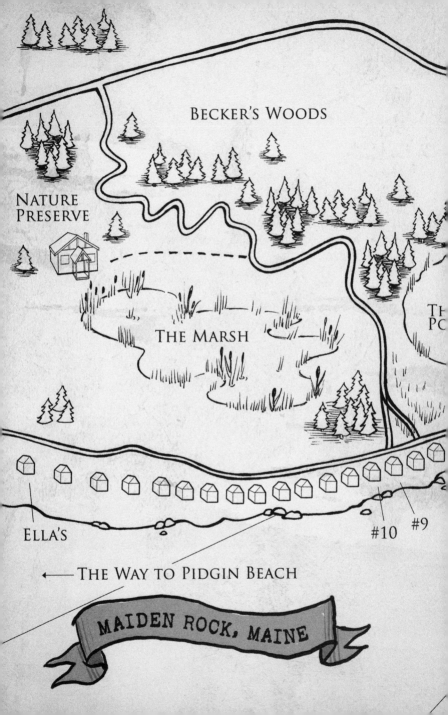

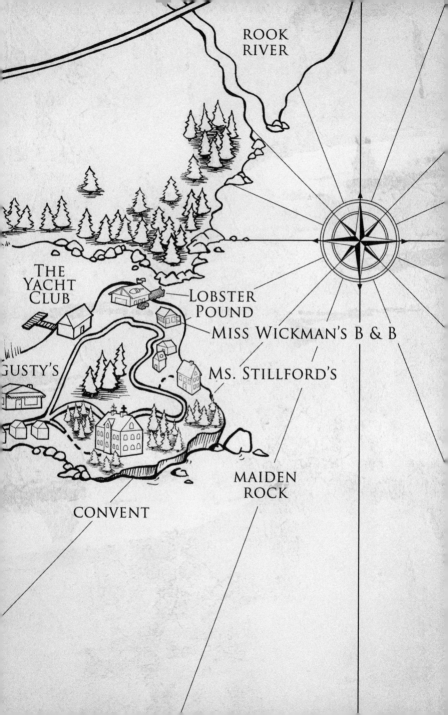

ROOK
RIVER

THE
YACHT
CLUB

LOBSTER
POUND

MISS WICKMAN'S B & B

GUSTY'S

MS. STILLFORD'S

MAIDEN
ROCK

CONVENT

I

"What time is it?" Ella asks again.

"It's thirty seconds later than the last time you asked."

I'm twisting my hair, and she's blowing on her nail polish.

"They should be here," she says.

It's May, and spring has finally found its way to the North Atlantic. The funky aroma of washed-up seaweed fills the air, and damp cold still seeps out of the wooden boards we're perched on. We've broken out the flip-flops and shorts but pulled hoodies on over our T-shirts. In Maine, spring means sixty-five-degree days, tops. The sun's weak, but we're sure it's giving us some color.

"Have they driven to New England before?" I ask her.

"Are you kidding?" Ella says. "I think this is the

first time they've ever driven anywhere."

Ella's waiting for her Aunt Ceil and Uncle Edgar. They're only sort of relatives, actually. But they've been her family's friends forever. They're coming for a vacation from being famous vampire-novel writers. Many of Ella's dad's writer friends have visited Maiden Rock, but until now it's been detective and spy types.

Ella—full name Mariella Philpotts—is the thirteen-year-old daughter of famous New York crime novelist Jack Philpotts. How can I describe Ella? First, let me say: shoes. She has a carnival of shoes in her closet. And, eyes: she has several fishing tackle boxes full of shadow and liner. Also, nails: dozens of little bottles of shimmering polish crowd her desk. And, of course, the blues: her nickname came out of her undying worship of Ella Marvell, "the uncontested queen of 1960s rhythm and blues."

When my best friend, Zoe, left for Scotland last fall, my heart ached. Up until then, the two of us had ruled our remote coastal town of Maiden Rock, Maine—along with Zoe's cousin, Ben. Zoe's leaving blew up normal. After Ella and her dad came to town, I couldn't imagine being friends with a girl who was so exotic, especially one that Ben was head-over-heels crushing over. (Yes, I was more than a tiny bit jealous.) But then I got to know her. And day by day, little by little, I found out she was okay. In fact, she was more than okay. She became a true friend.

For one thing, she helped me find my missing teacher, Ms. Stillford. And when no one else believed my theories, Ella stuck with me. And even though Ben was following her around like a puppy, she didn't make a big deal out of it. "Ella and Quinnie" was just as important to her as "Ella and Ben."

Three weeks before Zoe was supposed to come home for the summer, Zoe's dad decided to stay overseas for another year. The good news? Ella's dad liked Maiden Rock so much, he bought the old Sprague place at the end of the beach. Oh, Ella will always be more of a New Yorker than a Maiden Rocker, but that's okay. In fact, I rely upon her New Yorkiness whenever I need an honest assessment of someone.

As Ella waits for Edgar and Ceil Waterman, I'm waiting for the new people who are moving into Zoe's house. They have a thirteen-year-old boy, which is exciting news, since our vacation town is boy-bleak once the summer people leave after Labor Day.

The newbies' son is named Dominic. They have described him to my mom as "studious." Ella says that's code for "high geek factor." Sigh.

"My mom says the parents are professors of marine

biology," I tell her. "They're from New Jersey. That's pretty much the same as New York, right?"

"If they're from Newark, they could be teaching mutant biology. It's all fuel tanks in that place."

"Still, the son could be cool."

"I dunno. I smell a collection of Funko Pops coming nearer and nearer," Ella says as she applies a final coat of Darling Daffy Gold polish to her nails.

"Funko Pops?"

"*Geek* toys."

"And you know this because . . . ?"

"Because one of my dad's nerd fans kept sending them to him and telling Dad he should put them in one of his novels."

We're sitting on my steps at #10 Mile Stretch Road. Just like all the other beach houses, this side faces the street, and the other side faces the ocean. Behind us, also overlooking the street, is my mom's office, with three desks: her real estate-lady desk, her mayor's desk, and her sheriff's desk. Did I mention how small this town is? Oh, and Mom's the postmaster too.

"Girls?" The screen door to Mom's office creaks open. "You still want to help me with summer welcome packets?" She's dressed in her sheriff's uniform, which has super unflattering trousers, a weird, thick belt, and sturdy black shoes. But she's smiling in spite

4

of the clunky regulation footwear, so she must be having a good real-estate day.

I'm about to say, "Sure," when something catches my eye. A car has emerged from the woods at the far end of the access road. It's heading straight toward us, leaving a cloud of dust along the quarter mile between the woods and the beach. Ella gets on her feet, leaning to the left and then the right, trying to make out the passengers.

"I better get the keys for the Buttermans' place," Mom says, heading back into her office.

I call to her. "How do you know it's the science people?"

She calls back. "It's exactly 1:00 p.m., and they are science people. I'm figuring they're the ones who will be on time."

She's right.

A silver SUV pulls up to the front of our house, and two science parents get out. And a boy.

Not bad. Black T-shirt with a small pi symbol on the chest. Not-too-baggy jeans. Vans. Of course, there is the issue of the hat. He's wearing a flat-like-a-pancake, gray-and-brown plaid golf hat. It's the kind my grandpa has on in a photograph hanging in the upstairs hallway (except it doesn't have the pom-pom, thank goodness).

"Huh," Ella whispers. "Part geek, part vintage."

Mom walks up to the parents with her hand extended. I think she's forgotten she has her uniform on. They look at her like, *Uh-oh.*

"How do you do? I'm Margaret Boyd. Welcome to Maiden Rock."

"How do you do . . ."—the dad searches for a title—"uh, Officer?"

Mom looks down at her badge and laughs. "Ah. Yes, I'm also the sheriff. It's a small town."

They check out her holster as they take the keys from her.

"You're right next door to us," Mom says, pointing to Zoe's house. "Best location on the beach, and we always get plowed out first in the winter."

Dominic takes a step to the side, which happens to put him a few inches from me. I don't move away. He smells good. Like clean sheets.

"She doesn't carry her gun all the time," I reassure him. "She's got some police thing in Rook River this afternoon."

"That's cool," he says. "I feel very safe now."

"Girls?" Mom's voice snaps me back into the moment. "Could you help our new neighbors with their luggage?"

Ella looks at her nails, then tests one hand for

dryness with the back of the other. Dominic holds up his palm as if to say, *Save your nails. I got it.*

"Thanks, Margaret—Sheriff," says the dad. "We can handle it."

I am busy imagining what's in Dominic's bags—and hoping there are none of those Funko things—when I feel a breeze from Ella's direction. I look sideways, and she's rushing into the middle of the road, waving her arms like she's marshaling in a jumbo jet. A black sedan with dark windows emerges from a cloud of gravel dust and halts in front of her. The wheel wells are splattered with spring mud, but the rest of the car is rounded, sleek, and shiny. The passenger window powers down, and Ella leans in for a hug.

2

I wait for Ceil and Edgar to park the car and get out to meet Mom and me, but they don't.

Instead, Ella waves at me to get in the back-seat with her. I look for Mom, but she's talking to Biologist mom. Dominic has hoisted a suitcase up on his hip and he's hauling it up the steps. I run to the black sedan and jump in.

Ella is so excited; she's squeezing my hand and full-on smiling, which is rare for her. She usually keeps a cool thing going. She points down the road, and the car heads toward her house. I'm staring at the backs of two heads—one bald, one with the straight-est, blackest hair I've ever seen.

"This is my aunt Ceil," Ella says, touching Ceil's shoulder. "And this is my uncle Edgar." She pats his arm.

From where I'm sitting, I can't see Edgar's full face. Dark sunglasses sit on the bridge of a strong, pointed nose. A closely-trimmed white beard covers a set of sharp cheekbones. It's all anchored by a knob of an Adam's apple. He raises his hand in a kingly wave, and I notice his white, thin fingers and longish fingernails. Kind of *eeew*.

Ceil turns her head to me. Below her dark glasses, her face is pale and almost papery white, with dark, berry-red lips. She looks almost sickly, but when she cracks a weary smile, I can see that she's just tired. I guess if I spent all my time writing about bloodsuckers, I'd need some time off too.

When we reach Ella's house, her dad is waiting on the front porch.

"Edgar! Ceil! Come in, come in. So glad you're here."

"Oh, Jack," says Ceil as she hugs Mr. Philpotts, "what an ordeal."

"Driving out of the city can be like that," he says. "But just you wait. We drive everywhere here in the Down East."

"I don't know," says Edgar, "I'd like to put the car in the garage, pull down the door, and not look at it again for a long time."

"Well, come on in and stay awhile," says Mr. Philpotts. "Maiden Rock is the perfect place to rest and recharge."

"We'll carry all your stuff," Ella offers.

Ceil puts her arm around Ella's neck and pulls her close. It's sweet . . . except for Ceil's studded stiletto fingernails, which I wouldn't want anywhere near my jugular. Maybe this is where Ella gets her love of decorative nail features.

Ella loads me up with suitcases and tote bags, and we struggle upstairs to a big bedroom overlooking the ocean. Ceil is already up there, pulling the drapes shut to block the view. She catches me watching her as she pulls off her sunglasses.

"My eyes are tired, darlings." She rubs her temples, being careful not to poke herself in the eye with a fingernail. "Oh, that light, it's too much. I just need to rest."

I don't know how long a car trip from Brooklyn to Maine takes, but I imagine it's pretty tiring, especially when you don't drive very often.

Ella asks her if she needs anything . . . water, diet soda, tea?

"Coffee, El. I'd kill for a double espresso."

"I don't know," Ella says. "Maybe we can get it at Gusty's."

I look at her like she's crazy. Even her dad, the famous crime writer, who has been begging for stronger coffee at the café for nine months, has been unable to convince my dad, aka Gusty, to get an espresso machine.

Aunt Ceil is already stretched out on the bed in her black pants and black turtleneck, dragging an arm over her eyes when we close the door.

"We aren't going to be able to get a double espresso or any kind of espresso at Gusty's, and you know it," I tell Ella.

"I know. I just thought maybe now that there are three people who want it, maybe your dad would . . ."

"We'd have a better chance asking my mom. If anyone would want to please them, she would. They might buy a house here, like your dad did."

"That would be the coolest thing ever."

"I don't know. They're a little strange."

"They. Are. Not. They're just from Brooklyn."

              * * *

On the way to Gusty's Café, Ella explains that Brooklyn is a world where nobody is strange, because everybody is kind of strange.

"Is everybody in Brooklyn like Edgar and Ceil?"

"No, I'm telling you—you get to be whoever you are there."

"How many people are like Edgar and Ceil?"

"I don't know. A lot, maybe."

"I don't think I'll be going to Brooklyn any-time soon."

"You'll miss the Cyclone roller coaster at Coney Island."

"Oh, yeah? Just wait. This summer we'll go on the Galaxi at Old Orchard Beach." I feel pretty sure the Galaxi can beat the Cyclone.

The afternoon regulars are in Gusty's for plain old coffee.

Owen Loney, the lobsterman, is here with our wonderful teacher, Ms. Stillford, who became Blythe Stillford-Loney when the two of them secretly married a year ago. They kept it quiet for a while because they didn't want to upset Ben's uncle, John Denby, who has had a crush on Ms. Stillford forever. People really try and respect each other's feelings around here.

Ms. Stillford waves us over to her table, where she is reading *Transylvanian Drip* by Victoria Kensington, aka Ceil and Edgar. It's their new best seller about Count Le Plasma.

"Come, come, girls." She pastes what looks like the fiftieth sticky note on a page near the end. "Is Victoria Kensington here yet, Ella? Or should I say, are *they* here yet?"

"They *are*." Ella drops into a chair and rests her chin on her hands with a happy look on her face. "But they're resting. They need some time off."

"Well," says Ms. Stillford, "I'm eager to make their acquaintance."

"Maybe," Ella says. "My dad says they really want to fly under the radar."

Ms. Stillford laughs. "I'm sure Maiden Rock will respect their privacy, but please let them know that we'd all love to meet them. At their convenience. We want them to have a lovely visit."

Dad walks up at just the right time. "Can I get you girls anything?"

"Victoria Kensington wants double espressos," Ella says.

"What do you think, Gus?" Ms. Stillford adds. "Is it time to break down and get that espresso machine?"

Dad groans. "Oh, brother. I wonder if I can get by with one of those Nespresso makers or if I have to do the whole Italian steam job. But, hey, that's three strong coffee drinkers now. Right, Ella? Your dad and now your aunt and uncle."

"You can sign me up for a latte a day," Ms. Stillford says.

"Okay, okay. Such is the way of caffeinated prog-ress. But for today, what can I get you guys? And Ella, can I send some not-too-feeble Colombian home with you?"

"Sure," Ella says. "And I'll take a not–too–feeble Colombian with cream right now."

"Quinnie? Moxie?"

"Sure, Dad. And Cheese Nips."

"Okay, girls." I can tell by the tone of Ms. Stillford's voice, she's about to get down to business. "I have an idea." She's drumming her fingers on the cover of *Transylvanian Drip*. "We have only a few days of school left before summer break, and you've worked so hard all year. How about we spend the little time we have left—while our famous visitors are in town—reading and analyzing this book? We could do a compare and contrast with Bram Stoker's *Dracula*. We could maybe meet with the authors . . . if they are up to it, that is."

Ella is jumping out of her skin, she's so in love with this idea. I'm about to say, "Okay, sure," since I've already read *Transylvanian Drip*, when the café door opens and Mom leads the biologists and Dominic inside.

"Blythe," Mom says, walking them up to our table. "Let me introduce you to the Moldartos: Dr. James Moldarto, Dr. Mary Ann Moldarto, and I know you have been expecting Dominic."

I look at him standing there with his hands in his pockets, and I don't know who I feel sorrier for—Dominic, because he has to go to a new school for the last three days' worth of lessons, or me and Ella, because a new kid is invading our perfect private tutoring world. I'm guessing he'd rather be going to Rook River Middle School, like Ben, but he's stuck with us.

"Dominic, why don't you join our group?" Ms. Stillford steers Dominic into a seat next to me. "How much fun is this? A new student. We are going to have so much fun!"

"Hey," he says to me.

"Hey."

"We had a police escort down here," he says cheekily.

"I saw that."

"It made me feel very safe."

"Shut up." Okay. He's a little funny.

"Dominic," Ms. Stillford starts, "Ella and Quinnie and I were just talking about a possible project. Have you read Victoria Kensington's *Transylvanian Drip*, by any chance?" Ms. Stillford holds up Edgar and Ceil's book.

"Uh-huh," he says.

This is huge for Ella. She's looking at Dominic with new interest. She slyly winks at me. I realize she's sizing him up as good enough to be my boy-friend. His having read her aunt and uncle's book is a big plus.

"How about Bram Stoker's *Dracula*?" Ms. Stillford asks.

He nods. "Sure. Yeah. I've read it," he says.

"Excellent." Ms. Stillford beams at him. "How about you two?" she asks Ella and me.

"No," Ella says.

"Nope," I say. "Not *Dracula*."

Then Ms. Stillford gets that glint in her eye that means she's having teacher-kind-of-fun, and asks Dominic if he can list three defenses against vampires.

He laughs. "Sure. A crucifix. Garlic. And . . ." He looks like he's going to scratch his forehead, but instead he makes the sign of the cross and points two fingers at Ms. Stillford.

Ms. Stillford throws back her head and laughs so heartily, I think she might not catch her breath. What the heck? Dominic has been here five minutes, and now he and Ms. Stillford are talking in some kind of Dracula sign language.

Dominic leans back and looks a lot more comfortable. I glance sideways at his face. Under his golf hat, which I guess he never takes off, he has blue eyes and a friendly mouth with a slightly crooked smile.

Ms. Stillford starts talking about getting Ella and me copies of *Dracula* and how we'll do a comparison of the two books. She tells Dominic he can lead the first discussion. I think I hear him groan just a little bit. But now, I'm feeling a little more comfortable too. I realize that having another kid in our class spreads the work around.

# 3

Pretty soon, all the school talk around our café table fades, and Ms. Stillford and I start sharing Maiden Rock stories with Dominic.

"When Quinnie's dad was your age, he worked as a busboy right here in Gusty's. That was the second Gusty, I think," says Ms. Stillford. "It's been a Boyd family institution, right, Quinnie?"

"Oh, yeah? How many Gustys have there been?" Dominic asks.

"Three. My dad, his dad, and his dad." Then I add the phrase I've heard for years, "And they all made a wicked blueberry pie."

"But it was Gusty the Second who started the tradition of tossing French fries to the gulls," says Ms. Stillford. "Because they didn't have French fries before that. They had fried potatoes."

"Tossing fries to the gulls?" Dominic's left eyebrow

arches, tilting the brim of his hat.

"You'll see," says Ella. "Hey, wait a minute. There was a time without fries?"

"It was the olden days, dear," says Ms. Stillford. "Back when horses pulled wagons and we walked to school through blizzards with hot rocks in our pockets."

"Oh my gosh. The weather," Ella says. "Last winter, the snow was up above the kitchen window."

"Last winter was a bad one, I agree," says Ms. Stillford, "but not as harsh as the year we got clobbered with sixty-one inches. They had to bring in military trucks with plow heads the width of the road to dig us out."

Dominic has lost his amused expression, so I try to think of less daunting Maiden Rock tales. In my moment of hesitation, Ella jumps in. "There's a really old convent out on the point—"

"Ella!" I don't mean to snap at her, but she's about to talk about things we don't usually bring up in front of Ms. Stillford.

"What?" Ella charges right ahead. "The nuns there used to feed the feral cats and they had like a hundred of them." She looks at me like, *See? I'm not saying anything that I shouldn't say.*

"Whoa," Dominic says and widens his eyes. "I'd say I want to see that, but I'm not sure I want to see that."

"Oh, they aren't at the convent anymore," Ella says. "They run a cat rescue foundation in a lighthouse."

"It's actually a neat old place," I add, then stop myself from yapping on. He probably thinks we have so little to do here that seeing a bunch of feral cats in a crumbling lighthouse is a big deal.

"Well, I think it's time for me to get going." Ms. Stillford stands up and gathers her notes and Post-it tabbed copy of *Transylvanian Drip*.

I give Ella a now-look-what-you've-done glare, but she forges ahead in defiance. "The sisters—"

Owen Loney interrupts her before she can go any further, walking to the table and touching Ms. Stillford's elbow like he can tell she's ready to leave.

Ms. Stillford says, "Well, we're off. Girls and Dominic, I'll see you all bright and early Monday, and we'll talk about vampires." As they leave, I hear Owen Loney grumbling to Ms. Stillford about "vampire foolishness and whatnot."

Dad's at the table now, picking up the empty plates and cups. When I offer to bus our stuff myself, he says, "I've got it, Quinnie. I'm going to run another dish load. Looks like the afternoon pie rush is about to start."

I'm about to introduce Dominic to Dad when the café door opens and Sisters Ethel and Rosie bustle in.

Dad wipes the table. "See? Here come the sisters for their daily afternoon slice."

Those of us who live here are used to seeing the sisters in their old-fashioned nuns' habits, so I don't think anything of it, but I notice Dominic's surprise. They are "a couple of characters," as my mom calls them. The tall, thin one is Sister Ethel—full name Sister Ethelburga—and has a face like a wrinkled apple-head doll. Sister Rosie—full name Sister Maria Giuseppe Rossello—is short, round, and bouncy. She loves cats, hot chocolate, and mini-Snickers bars. She also drives their white van like a speed demon, which makes my mom crazy.

The sisters were the last two nuns to depart the old Our Lady of the Tides Convent. All the others passed away over the years. Now they run the cat rescue on Pidgin Beach just south of here, while a younger nun is working to turn the old convent building into the Maiden Rock Spiritual Center. Sisters Ethel and Rosie took the demotion with dignity, but given the circumstances, which we don't talk about much, they didn't really have a choice.

On the way to their regular seats at the counter, they stop at our table.

"Hi, Sisters," Ella says. "This is Dominic. He's new."

"Oh, hello, Dominic," bubbles Sister Rosie. "Welcome. Where are you from?"

I can tell Dominic didn't expect to have to talk to the sisters. He straightens up in his seat.

"We're from New Jersey. And we're living next to . . ." He looks at me and blanks on my name. This is not a good start.

"Us," I say. "His family is living in the Buttermans' house this year."

"Oh, they're not coming back?" Sister Rosie makes a pouty face on my behalf, because she knows how much I miss Zoe. Then she turns back to Dominic. "What do your parents do?"

"They're marine biologists. They're going to teach at the college in Rook River for a year."

"Do they like cats?" Sister Rosie goes right for the cat placement opportunity.

"Rosie, give the boy a chance to eat his first piece of pie before you try to get him to adopt," says Sister Ethel.

"Ella's aunt and uncle are here too," I say.

"Yeah, but they're resting. They need some time off," Ella says.

"The ones who wrote that book?" says Sister Rosie. A small wrinkle appears between her eyes.

Ella brightens. "*Transylvanian Drip*. Did you read it?"

"Yes, dear," says Sister Rosie. "I think everyone around town has read it, since we all heard they were coming. Will they be signing it here at Gusty's?"

"Did you love it?" Ella asks.

Sister Rosie wrings her hands. "Well, I wish they hadn't been so mean to the cat."

Ella's face falls. She looks to Sister Ethel for support. "It's just a story," Ella says. "It didn't really happen."

"Sister Rosie knows that, Ella," says Sister Ethel. "She's just sensitive about the kitties. Right, Rosie? You're not saying it wasn't a good book."

Before Sister Rosie can elaborate, Dad waves the sisters over to the counter.

"Two blueberry pies and two coffees," he calls out.

Ella looks bummed. I can tell she's taking Sister Rosie's criticism personally.

"It was a unique detail," Dominic says. "Who would have thought to kidnap a pedigreed cat for blood ransom?"

"They don't hurt the cat," Ella says a little peevishly.

The truth is I've only skimmed the book. I didn't read every single word. I'm not a big vampire fan.

I didn't even read all of *Twilight* when the whole world was gaga over it. I watched the movie, though. It was okay.

"Have a drink of my Moxie," I tell Ella, trying to distract her. I know she hates Moxie.

She perks up and looks at the can. "No, Dominic, you drink it. You won't be a real *Mainah* until you learn to love this stuff. And try and deny that it tastes like toothpaste!"

Ella holds the can up to his lips. As Dominic attempts to take a sip and not let her spill it on him, Ben walks through the café door. I guess he didn't have practice today. No sweat or shower hair.

I look at Ben. He looks at Ella and Dominic. His head tilts a little like he's trying to understand what's going on, and there's the tiniest flicker of concern in his eyes.

# 4

Ella sees Ben and her face lights up. In a second, she pulls a chair up between her and Dominic and pats the seat for Ben to sit. Ben's concern dissolves and he slouches into the chair.

"Want to read *Dracula* with us this week?" Ella asks him.

She has to be kidding.

Ben's expression turns from relief to dread. "But I read the Transylvania book."

It's clear he would rather eat worms than read any more vampire books. Ben likes running, playing baseball, and weird scientific details. Ella laughs. "Never mind."

Dad is at our table again, asking if the guys want anything.

"I'll have a milk, thanks," Ben answers.

"This is Dominic," I tell Dad.

"Hey, Dominic. How's it going? I just met your parents." Dad tips his head toward the table where Mom is showing the Moldartos a map of the Maine coast. "What can I get you?"

"Give him a Moxie too," says Ella. "It's a rite of passage."

"Coming right up," Dad says.

As Dad walks away, I open my mouth to say that Moxie is really good, but Ben interrupts me to say, "Vampires are science fiction. I'd rather read real science."

"Meet Ben," I say to Dominic. "He's a walking Wikipedia."

Ben smiles as if he approves of the description. "It's all made-up," he continues. "Science fiction is for kids."

"Some of the best stuff ever written for adults is sci-fi," Dominic replies, almost scoffing. The tension soars.

Ella and I share glances in a cone of uncomfortable silence. Are these two guys, who've barely said "hey" to each other, going to have a science–versus–science fiction smackdown right here?

Ella puts her hand on Ben's arm. "Ben, Dominic's family just moved into Zoe's house."

The guys consider each other. Well, I realize, now I know a little more about Dominic. He's not the kind of guy who backs down when he believes in something. I just wish that *something* wasn't sci-fi.

And then Dominic starts the argument again. "Stephen Hawking thinks there are aliens. He's about as scientific as they come."

Ben laughs. "I know that." He whispers to Ella, "It's a ten-year scientific search for life beyond Earth. It's called Breakthrough Listen."

"I'm just saying," says Dominic, "why look for something you think isn't there?"

Ben says, "Maybe to disprove that it's there, so people can stop imaging they've had their brains probed." He turns back to Ella. "Do your aunt and uncle think vampires are real?"

Ella looks confused. When did the conversation become about who believes in vampires?

"I don't know," Ella says. "They say they're retelling Count Le Plasma's actual life as he tells it to them, but I kind of figure that's just part of the whole thing. You know. The fans like it."

"Really?" I stifle a laugh. "The vampire tells them stuff and they write it in the novels?"

"It's on the back of all the books, Quinnie." Ella's getting mad. She is seriously touchy about them.

"People have believed stranger things that turned out to be true," Dominic says, once again looking at Ben. "Like how the earth revolves around the sun . . ."

Ben stands up. "Nice to meet ya, Dominic, but I gotta go." This is Ben-speak for, *Dominic, I think you're kind of a jerk*. With that, he walks toward the café door.

"Wait, Ben." Ella gets up and follows him, but not before giving me big, accusing eyes, which I resent, because I'm not the one who ticked off Ben.

Dad reappears and puts the Moxie, the milk, and two strong coffees *to go* on the table, plus a refill on the Cheese Nips. "Where are Ben and Ella?"

"They had to leave," I say.

"I don't think I can recall a time when Ben didn't eat or drink free food," Dad says.

"I'll drink the milk and the soda," Dominic volunteers. "But not the coffee."

"No!" Dad and I say at the same time and shake our heads in unison.

"We don't mix milk and Moxie 'round these parts," Dad says and walks away with the glass.

Dominic reaches for a fistful of Cheese Nips and shakes them into his mouth. Orange crumbs fall to the table, and he brushes them into a mound with the back of his hand. "Mmm," he says. "These are good."

An important question works its way to the front of my mind. I decide it needs to be asked. "So, let's get this straight. Just how sci-fi are you?"

"What do you mean?"

I want to scream out, *How much of a geek?*, but I say, "Do you dress up like Yoda and go to conventions?"

He laughs. It's a nice laugh. His eyes get drawn into it. He has straight teeth like he's had braces. "No. No Yoda costumes."

"*Any* costumes?"

"No Yoda, no stormtrooper, no Kylo Ren. No costumes."

"Any hand signals?" I raise my hand and try to make the Mr. Spock *V.*

"That's *Star Trek*, and no. No hand signals." He pats down my hand. "Stop that, you suck at it."

"How about those little dolls? The Funko-things?"

He sits up and gets really serious. "Quinnie. That's your name, right? Quinnie?"

I nod.

"Yes. I have a collection of Funko Pops. They have serious monetary value, by the way. I have the full *Star Wars* vinyl collection, the Wolf Man, zombie Merle Dixon, and zombie Bicycle Girl, plus a few *Game of Thrones* my uncle gave me. You would like

Bicycle Girl. If that makes me a geek, then yes, I'm geek and I'm proud."

I'm not sure what to say. He's just owned up to geekiness. And he doesn't care who knows. It makes me wonder exactly what's so bad about geekiness in the first place. But I do have one more question. I point to the pi on his T-shirt. "Do all of your T-shirts have mathematical symbols?"

He tilts his head like he's thinking through the vast number of shirts he owns. "Yep. Well, either math or something A/V-related."

"You make videos?"

"No. I'm just seriously into the equipment . . . Yes, I make videos."

"Of what?"

"Lots of things," he says. "The stuff in my room."

This is too much. "What do you film in your room?"

"My stuff."

"Funko Pops and sci-fi stuff?"

"No, I have lots of different stuff. I'm a very diverse person. I even have some vampire stuff. There's definitely a Nosferatu Funko Pop on my shelf."

"Do you have alien stuff?"

"I may have some alien stuff," he says.

"But you don't believe in aliens?"

"Not sure."

"Or vampires?"

"Probably not. But you don't have to believe in stuff to think it's cool."

He's right about that. And that makes him so different from Ben. "Is that why you read *Transylvanian Drip*?"

"No. My parents made me read it," Dominic says, "because your mother told them that Victoria Kensington was here and we'd get to meet her."

"Victoria Kensington is a *them*: Edgar and Ceil."

"I know that now."

"Do you want to meet them?"

"Sure."

"Then let's go take them this superstrong coffee."

# 5

I tell Dad we'll take the cups of Colombian to the Philpotts' house, and he says, "Great. They just called in an entire meal order, complete with 'mind-crushing' coffee, so I'll make a really strong pot."

In seconds, Mom is at my shoulder. I swear she has radar like a bat. She can hear every conversation in a room, even while she's busy showing people a map, talking on her phone, and checking the speed of the sisters' van as it leaves the parking lot.

"Quinnie, drop off the coffee and food, but do not—I repeat, *do not*—bother Edgar and Ceil. They are here for a relaxing vacation. They want privacy."

"But Dominic wants to meet them."

"I'm sure he will, but not until they're ready. I've spoken to Jack Philpotts, Quinnie. They want to be left alone."

"But when they come to Gusty's, can we—"

"They won't be coming to Gusty's. They've arranged for daily deliveries."

There are about ten things I want to whine about right now, the first of which is, *How weird is that?*

"Work with me on this, Quinnette. Can you do that? The summer people will start arriving any day now, and I need your help. This is important."

After hearing that, what am I supposed to do?

"Sure, Mom. I'll help." Saying it feels better than I thought it would. I don't even roll my eyes.

Mom squeezes my shoulder like she's proud of me. I'm kind of proud of me too. I could have argued with her. I *would have* argued with her a year ago.

Dominic had stepped back during my lecture from Mom. He's standing with his parents, a few tables away.

Mom looks at him and says to me, "You two take the delivery to the Philpotts' house. Then you can show Dominic around Maiden Rock."

When I tell him this, his parents think it's a *splendid* idea and add that they are going to "hit the beach to gather crustal brines and other specimen."

"Crustal brines?" I ask Dominic.

He whispers, "I'll explain later. It's an oceanography-ichthyology thing."

For a second, he looks like the parent of kids who can't wait to play in the sand.

* * *

Dominic and I stand in the Gusty's parking lot, with me juggling a bag packed with lobster rolls, chowder, and blueberry pie in one hand, and a napkin full of cold French fries in the other. Dominic is clutching a large thermos full of strong coffee. He squats and ducks as I toss the fries into the air for the circling gulls. One of the gulls, I recognize on sight: it's old, scarred-up Buster. He never misses a fry. I make a few hard-to-catch tosses and give up a few easy ones. After the gulls have swooped and snapped and caw-cawed their thanks, they pinwheel away.

"I can skip the gull interaction excursion next time." Dominic straightens up and checks to make sure his hat is secure.

"It's tradition. Plus, they're just leftovers. The gulls might as well eat them," I say.

"I'm surprised Ben hasn't told your dad about saturated fats and the effect upon the avian body mass index," Dominic says.

I look at him, trying to figure out if he's jabbing at

34

Ben, and if he is, whether it's because of science–versus–sci-fi or something else—like Ella. I decide it's neither. Just standard new-kid competitiveness. I see it every summer with the vacation kids. It especially shows up at sailing lessons. Fortunately for everyone's water safety, the conflicts work themselves out in a couple weeks.

"Ben's given his two cents," I say, "but Dad doesn't use saturated fats to cook his fries, so . . ." I raise my shoulders in the so-what salute.

We're walking south from Gusty's, past the Buttermans'—the Moldartos' for the next twelve months—then past our house and down the road, toward Ella's, which is the last house on the beach at the end of the road.

"What's the big secret?" Dominic asks.

"What secret?"

"The writers. Why do we have to bring them food? Why can't they come to the café like everybody else?"

I give him the explanation that's been given to me. "They're famous and they want to be left alone for a while. They don't want people bugging them for autographs or whatever. That's all."

"Sheesh. How famous are they? They can't make a cup of coffee?"

"Oh, famous-famous. Do you know about Ella's dad? Jack Philpotts? He writes crime books. He's famous too. And he can't make a cup of coffee either. I mean, he can *make* it, but Ella says it tastes like motor oil."

"Nope. Never heard of him."

"You've heard of Stephen King?"

Dominic stops dead and looks at me with his eyes bugged out. "Is Ella's dad Stephen King?"

I bust out laughing. "No. Duh. I'm just saying Ella's dad is *like* Stephen King, except he writes crime stories, not horror. And Edgar and Ceil are even more famous than Ella's dad. So they want some time off from being celebrities."

"Do they really say they get their stories directly from the vampire, Count Le Plasma?"

"That was news to me. I only read the one book and"—I keep walking and don't look at Dominic—"I only skimmed it."

"That's okay. I'm not huge into vampires either. It would have been cooler if they wrote about were-wolves. Or zombies." He widens his eyes, stiffens his arms, and staggers a few feet.

"You like zombies?" I ask.

"Zombies, werewolves, all kinds of gory stuff. Plus *The Strain*. I love *The Strain*. It's all great. But do

I stay up at night, worrying they're going to break into my room and suck my brains out? No."

I laugh so hard I almost drop the bag of food. "What's *The Strain*?"

"It's a show about vampirism, but—! It's being caused by a virus that's passed from person to person, like any other infection."

"Eeww! Gross!"

"It's called Code V or V5."

"Not *really*."

"Yes, it's *really* called that. And it's not just in the show—people have real-life theories about that kind of thing. You can read about it online. Nobody's ever *disproved* it."

I look at this boy walking next to me, carrying coffee, and spouting off about V5. He's so easygoing about who he is. Geek and proud. He's hilarious.

"If we have to walk much farther, I'm going to break into this thermos. It smells really good," Dominic says.

"You do and you'll have to answer to some serious coffee lovers."

"If they even let me see them."

"Oh, I hope you get to see them. The guy's got, like, *long* fingernails."

"How long?"

"Long like a woman's," I say. "And Ceil's finger-nails were long and pointy and deep red. And so were her lips."

"Her lips were long and pointy?"

"Her *fingernails*. Dummy!"

Dominic smiles but doesn't totally concede that he was being stupid on purpose.

## 6

It's getting to be late afternoon, and the sun is the hottest it's going to be for the day. The temperature has struggled upward, but a chilly wind is blowing in from across the ocean. I'm wishing I had jeans on instead of shorts.

"When does it warm up around here?" Dominic asks. I think he's looking at the goose bumps on my legs.

"In a couple weeks, it will be warmer."

"Like go-in-the-water warmer?"

"The water never gets over sixty or so here. So that's what we call warm."

"I guess it doesn't matter, really," Dominic says. "Jersey's got a shore. But we don't actually go swimming very much. Mostly my parents take samples from it."

I'm trying to walk in step with him, but I'm having a hard time. I try to take bigger steps and match up, but then I think he's trying to slow down and let me catch up. First I lag, then he lags. I decide to just walk my walk, and we go along.

"Was that their car that drove in after us? The one with the tinted windows?"

"Yes. That was their car."

"It was a seriously great car."

By now, we're standing in front of Ella's. The ocean breeze should be whooshing around her house and smacking us in the face, but I swear the gusts are blowing from the opposite direction, from across the marsh behind us, pushing us a step closer to her door.

"Did you hear that?" Dominic asks.

"The creaking?"

"Yeah, like old boards straining against the wind."

"That's exactly what it is. Welcome to Maiden Rock. All of these places are old. Old and creaky."

"Where's the car?" Dominic asks.

"In the garage. Come on, let's get the food inside while the chowder and coffee are still hot."

Dominic is already at the old wooden garage door, shading his eyes to see through the four dirty square windows along the top. He whistles. "This is not just a car."

"What do you mean?" I jump to see in the window but I'm a few inches too short.

"It's exactly what I thought it was."

"Which is what?"

"A Flying Spur."

"What's a Flying Spur?"

"It's a Bentley. It's magic. And it can go like the wind."

"How do you know this?"

"Because a famous vampire drove a Flying Spur."

"Oh, yeah?" I ask. "What famous vampire?"

"You are so busted."

"What? Why?"

Dominic smirks. "Because the famous vampire who drove a Flying Spur was Count Le Plasma. And you are lucky that *I* outed you instead of Ella."

He's right. I am lucky. She would have been super mad about me skimming the book, which reminds that me she *was* kind of mad when she followed Ben out of Gusty's.

"Come on," I tell Dominic, "they're waiting."

I march up to the Philpotts' front door and knock, wondering if Ella will even open the door. Dominic stands behind me like a butler, pulled-up all straight and dignified, holding the thermos.

Ella's dad greets us, not Ella herself, so I still don't know whether Ella's holding a grudge.

"I've been expecting you, young lady," Jack

Philpotts says. "Your dad called and said he was going to get an espresso maker."

"Great," I say. I feel pretty sure that Mom weighed in on this.

"I told him I'd spring for the overnight delivery charges."

I look at Mr. Philpotts to see if he's making a joke or he really plans to pay for the delivery. It's hard to tell with him. I decide to smile and say, "I know how much you love your coffee."

"Damn straight," he says and reaches for the thermos.

"Is Ella home?" I ask. I position myself to walk in once he says, *She's upstairs.*

"Nope," Mr. Philpotts replies. "She and Ben are on the beach. You can probably find them there."

I notice a shuffle behind me and realize I've forgotten to introduce Dominic. "Mr. Philpotts, this is Dominic. His family just moved into the Buttermans'."

"Hey there, Dominic," Jack Philpotts says. "That's a good location. We lived there for nine months. Nice beachfront."

Dominic falters like he doesn't know if he should extend a hand to the famous author, what with Mr. Philpotts's arms being full of takeout. "Yeah, I guess we get plowed out first."

"That you do," Mr. Philpotts says. "Well, see you, kids."

He closes the door, and I hear him call out, "Ceil, the coffee's here. Edgar?"

I give Dominic a wave. "This way. I'll show you the beach."

We walk around the Philpotts' house. From here, unlike my family's place, you have to climb a small dune and some rocks to get to the beach.

The North Atlantic is dark and deep with a silvery sheen across the surface. You know just by looking at it that if you put your leg in, it will send shivers clear through to your bone. Yet we spot four people there, knee-deep in the surf.

Ben and Ella are pushing each other as the low tide rolls across their shins. Ella laughs and tries to make Ben fall in, while Ben grunts, hopping to stay on his feet. When they see us, Ella walks out of the water toward me.

"Quinnie! Come in! It's great."

For about a second, I consider whether I should be leading Dominic anywhere near Ben. Then I think, *Hey, what's gonna happen will happen.*

"I'm coming!" I yell and run to the water, shedding my flip-flops along the way and then stomping in the surf.

When I'm good and soaked through, I look up for Dominic. He's sitting on top of a huge rock, with his elbows resting on his knees. I wave at him to come in, but he shakes his head.

"Come on!" I scream at him and splash some water.

Ella looks his way and yells, "It's great!"

Dominic scoots to the edge. I think he's going to ditch his shoes and hat and join us. But he doesn't. He jumps down and heads up to dry sand, toward the other two people up the beach—his parents. Poor guy. He doesn't have his beach legs yet. And he's getting sand inside his shoes. It's kind of painful to watch. Give him a month and he'll blend in . . . maybe.

I spread my arms and let the cool salty air—now blowing from the correct side of the universe—kiss my skin.

"You know I don't think your aunt and uncle are weird, right?" I ask Ella.

"I know," she says, then messes up my hair even more than the wind has.

It's a necessary fib, because I truly think "Brooklyn" doesn't begin to explain them. But she loves them, so I will like them.

I splash Ella a few more times before running down the beach after Dominic.

The Moldartos have set large plastic tackle boxes out on the sand. Tiers of small test tubes line the insides of the boxes, with a colored plastic cork in each tube. One tier has red corks, one yellow, one green, and on and on.

Mrs. Doctor Moldarto puts little snips of seaweed into yellow-corked tubes and labels them, while Mr. Doctor fills red-corked tubes with seawater. Dominic is raking the sand with his fingers.

"Hey!" He hands his mother a small crab, holding it by the back of its golden yellow body while its small, intricate legs and claws fidget in the air, trying to scurry sideways from danger.

Dominic's mom grabs a tube with an air-hole stopper and drops in the crab. She and Mr. Doctor exchange words like *hippoidea* and *ocypodinae*.

Dominic turns to me and says, "I've got to go make dinner. Wanna come?"

I look at my phone, and it's somehow become five fifteen. I know Mom will be home soon, and Dad will be turning the café over to the night manager, Clooney Wickham. Clooney is the twin sister of Miss Wickham, the owner of our local B&B. She comes every summer from Auburn to help out nights and Sundays and enjoy some summer vacation in her free time.

"I can't."

We walk up to the platform between our two houses and climb the four wooden steps. I imagine Dominic in the kitchen, cooking while his parents are absorbed in their research samples. I've never cooked for my family, what with my dad being a chef and all. We usually eat at the café or he brings café food home. I take that back. I make great toast.

"What's your phone number?" Dominic asks me and takes out his phone to type it in.

I put out my hand like, *give*, and he hands the phone over. "Now send me a text and I'll yoink yours," I tell him.

A second ago I was chilly, but this number-sharing warms me up. Before he can say anything, I reach up and grab his hat. He grabs it back and pulls it back in place.

A lot of guys would have been mad about this, but not Dominic. "I see you covet my hat," he says. "Well, maybe, if you're a good Maiden Rock tour guide, I'll let you try it on."

I get the teeniest inkling that under certain circumstances . . . if he doesn't do something really weird . . . and if the number of Funko Pops is not horrifying . . . I could fall into crushland.

# 7

I'm sitting on my bed at nine o'clock, reading my emails on my tablet and—yay!—there's one from Ms. Stillford. I open it and find a link to download Bram Stoker's *Dracula*.

I know I'm going to have to re-read, or rather, *really* read *Transylvanian Drip*, but for now, I might as well read *Dracula*. It's old. It's probably hokey. Maybe it'll be funny.

The story starts with Jonathan Harker, who is an English real estate man, bringing papers all the way to Transylvania for Count Dracula. Real estate people really went the distance for their clients in those days. I wonder if Mom has read this?

By nine thirty, it's getting dark, so I put my head down but keep reading. And it gets later, and I keep reading. And it gets later, and the coach driver who takes Jonathan to the Count's castle turns into a wolf that then turns into the Count. The castle gets creepier, and soon I notice that it's gotten really cold in my room. Maine nights normally get cold, but this is uncomfortable—as if the chill in the Count's castle is seeping into my house. I slip out of my covers, dash across the room, grab some socks and a fleece, and bolt back to bed.

I'm fumbling to get the clothes on under the covers when I feel a pressure in my ears. Like the ocean rhythm that rocks me to sleep every night has been replaced with static. Not loud. Just a low crackle.

But I can't stop reading because I have to finish this book tonight so I can read *Transylvanian Drip* tomorrow and be ready by Monday to discuss, compare, and contrast.

When my tablet says it's midnight, Count Dracula has started to give old Jonathan orders about where he can go in the castle, which of course Jonathan ignores. Why do victims always do that? He tries and tries to get out, but the Count has locked him in. He's doomed. My heart is kind of breaking for him. Jonathan's going to have his blood sucked for sure.

The salty air coming through the bedroom window has plastered my bangs to my forehead. I keep scooping them out and fluffing them up.

The next part of *Dracula* is prickles-on-the-back-of-your-neck creepy. Jonathan goes through some dark passageways and then—I can't believe this—into the vault with the Count. I can't scooch any farther under my covers. I think I hear a wolf howling. No. That's crazy. Wait. Are there are wolves in Maine? There are *bears* in Maine . . .

This is too, too, too scary. I set the tablet aside and pull the quilt over my head. I'll read again when it's light.

But I can't bring myself to close my eyes. I lie in bed for I don't know how long, thinking about bloody fangs and horrifying castle hallways.

That's it. I decide I'm better off awake, so I pick up the tablet and read on. Jonathan grabs a shovel and, lifting it high, smashes it into the Count's hateful face. The Count's head turns and gives Jonathan a "grin of malice which would have held its own in nethermost hell." *Nethermost* hell. Hmm. I assume that means the deepest, helliest part.

This, this, *this* is why I don't like vampire stories! And I'm only on page fifty-five!

I throw off my covers and jump out of bed, running around my room. I flail my arms to scare away the demons, pick up my phone, and start to text.

Me: *I am freaking out here!*

I don't expect him to answer. I'm pretty sure he's sleeping and totally clueless that right next door, I'm being pursued by vampires in my head. Then, yay!

Dominic: *What page are you at?*

Me: *50 freaking 5! Only 55!*

Dominic: *Oh man. Just wait.*

Me: *Great. More gore.*

Dominic: *Walk on the beach?*

Me: *Now? It's 3:30!*

Dominic: *Still just the beach. I'll protect you from the mutant crabs if you protect me from the ninja seaweed monsters.*

I laugh. Once I was on the beach a little past midnight at a Fourth of July bonfire. And I've been on the beach at five in the morning with Dad to dig clams, but in the middle of the night? The very middle-middle of the night? Nope. Not me. Until now.

Me: *I'll meet you at the top of the beach steps.*

Dominic: *In a flash.*

* * *

I'm crouched down in the marsh grass at the top of the steps, squinting in the direction of his house, and Dominic startles me by standing up from a hunched position a few feet away.

"Sheesh, scare me much!" I whisper.

"Quiet," he whispers back.

We know that if any of our parents catch us, we'll be jerked back inside by our hoodie strings. The temperature has dropped into the teeth-chattering range. I've got jeans and a sweatshirt, Top-Siders, *and* socks. Dominic is dressed warm too. But still, under his hood is the hat. Maybe he sleeps in it. *Naw.* He wouldn't do that. Please, no. *That* would be the too-weird thing.

The wooden stairs creak. They must creak all the time, but at three thirty a.m., you really hear it.

We pick up our pace and walk down the shore-line, heading in the direction of Ella's place, watching the surf bash the sand.

"I've smelled the beach often enough, with my parents always foraging, but this place has a stronger odor," Dominic says.

"I think it's the outcroppings. The big piles of rocks that form points beyond the tide line."

"I don't think rocks smell."

"Not the rocks," I say. "It's all the stuff that lives— and dies—between them, like seaweed and crabs and fish and gull droppings. Mix that with salt water, and it's pretty stinky. The pool is even worse because it almost drains twice a day."

"Right, Maiden Rock Tidal Pool. I've been hearing about it for days. My parents can't wait to get their waders on and start taking specimens there."

We're kicking sand as we make our way, and I'm trying to be a good example of how you keep it out of your shoes.

As we pass beach house after beach house, I get into the rhythm of calling out the names of the houses or the people who own them: Two Gulls, Crow's Nest, the Muellers, the Spencers—and then something moves in the clump of beach grass to our right.

I jump. "What was that?"

Dominic jumps too. "I don't know. Ready to go back?"

I look at the dune. The grass is still. Whatever was in there must have run the other way. "Just a few more houses and we're at the end. Then we can turn around."

We're about to turn around at Ella's house. My eyes have adjusted to the contrast between the dark ocean and the moonlight. Ahead of us lies the large outcropping that separates Maiden Rock from Pidgin Beach.

"Hey, look!" Dominic says.

"What? Where?"

"Up on the rocks. There's a dog up there."

"No way. Those rocks are slippery."

"No, look now!"

I stretch my neck to see where he's pointing, and Dominic's right. Something's moving up over the rocks. It's about the size of a German shepherd.

"That is so strange. Nobody in Maiden Rock has a dog like that."

Then I remember how I thought I heard a wolf howl when I was scaring myself silly reading *Dracula*. And *then* I remember how in *Dracula*, the Count turned into a wolf when Jonathan was in the coach on the way to the castle . . .

"This is way too creepy for me. That could be a wolf. And that wolf . . . could be . . . a vampire!" I pretend to raise my claws and bare my fangs. "Anyway, there are probably wolves in Becker's Woods."

"Let's go before it catches our scent and comes back to suck our blood," Dominic says.

Which starts us covering laughs and running and dodging between the water and the shore.

But when I get back in my room, I can't stop thinking about how the animal on the beach might be a wolf.

I pick up my tablet again. The story's where I left it, at page fifty-five. I scroll, search, and find the word *wolf* over and over. In fact, the Count turns into a wolf another time, when he travels by sea to England. When the ship docks, the crew's gone, the captain's dead, and a "large dog" is seen leaping from the deck—that wolf again.

And when I put down my tablet one last time, I can't breathe through the thought that a wolf could be as close as the edge of town.

# 8

I wake up at seven and really feel my lack of sleep: eyes sore from reading by tablet light most of the night, shoulders tense from what we saw on the beach.

*A dog. Just a dog.*

Or it could have been a wolf.

And that could mean a vampire might have been in the neighborhood.

*Shut up.*

But vampires were so vivid in *Dracula*, like it was an actual, for-real journal.

*Stupid. Stupid. Stupid.*

This is why a person should not read scary stuff in the middle of the night.

I shake my head, get up, and get dressed, and prepare to run downstairs and tell Mom about a possible wolf sighting on the rocks between our beach and

Pidgin Beach. Until I realize the first question she'll ask is, *Where and when?*

Still, I want to know what we saw. So I consider another approach.

She's sitting at the kitchen table, her favorite apple butter–and–cheese toast on a plate in front of her.

"I'm trying to figure out how to use this body cam the state gave me yesterday," Mom says. She's spread a small box and instruction pages out on the table. Something the size of a deck of cards is nested inside the box, waiting to turn on and record a crime.

"Cool. You're going to be like the police on TV. Do you have to wear it all the time?" I reach for it.

"Don't touch it. I have to read all that paperwork and get it set up."

I imagine her making a traffic stop on Mile Stretch Road. Oh, man. She always stops the sisters because they are always speeding. She'll get a recording of Sister Rosie trying to talk her way out of a ticket. Sister Rosie won't want the monsignor to see that!

"Do you have to tell people they're on camera?" I ask.

"Nope, and I can turn it on whenever I need to . . . while I'm on duty, that is."

"You're on duty all the time."

"I'm on duty whenever I need to be."

"So, even me? I'm going to be on camera?"

"What are you worried about?" She smiles. "You never do anything you wouldn't want me to see, right?" She takes a bite of her toast and studies my reaction.

"Stop it," I tell her. "Mom, are there wolves in Maine?"

"What?"

"I think I heard one howling last night."

"Around here? I don't think so. But why don't you ask John Denby. He'll know." She flips the instructions over like she can't find an answer. "I know there *are* coyotes."

"Here? There are coyotes here in Maiden Rock?"

"Just about a month ago, I saw one on the side of the road. It had been hit by a car."

"Aw."

"Yep. Skinny thing. Looked like it had late-winter starvation." Mom takes a drink of coffee. "I called it in to Animal Control. Now what are you up to today?"

It occurs to me that I have a ton of things to do. "I have to finish reading *Dracula* and re-read *Transylvanian Drip* and show Dominic more of Maiden Rock. And maybe I'll ask John Denby about wolves, or if there could be another coyote around."

"Mmm-hmm, good." She's deep in thought as she places the body cam on her shirt. I'd say she didn't hear a word of what I just said, but I know better. She probably got every bit of it.

Still, I can't resist testing Mom. "And then I'm going to drive Ceil and Edgar's Flying Spur to Old Orchard Beach and ride the Galaxi until I throw up."

"Oh, yeah?" she says without looking up. "Be home by five, okay?" She adjusts the body cam again. "What's a Flying Spur?"

"It's the fancy car that Ceil and Edgar drive—that Count Le Plasma drives too."

"Is that a real car name?" She looks up like she's mentally checking her motor vehicle database.

"Uh-huh. Dominic says it costs three hundred thousand dollars."

"Hmm. I don't know about that." She angles her shoulder toward me. "Say cheese."

I scream, duck, and run. "Going to the café for breakfast."

"Love you!"

"Love you too."

It's eight thirty on Saturday morning, and normally

I would be going to Gusty's with Ella and Ben would be joining us before he goes off to baseball practice. But when I walk out of the house, there's no Ella coming down the road toward me. I look over at Dominic's house, and his parents are packing up their SUV with specimen boxes.

"Headed to the tidal pool?" I call to them, trying to hide a smile. "You don't have to drive there. It's just across the street. Up there." I point in the direction of Gusty's.

"Oh, we know, honey. We just have so much gear, and we want to approach it from different access points as the tide is going out and coming in." Dominic's mom closes the back door of the car with a wham.

"Great!" I say. I'd warn her about all the strange and ugly sea life that gets stranded in the muck as the tide goes out, but then I realize that's exactly why she's so excited to go.

"Dominic says you're showing him the rest of town today," she says.

"Uh-huh."

"You kids have fun," says Mr. Moldarto.

They climb in the car and pull out, heading up toward the Maiden Rock Yacht Club, and Dominic comes out of the house.

59

"What's on the tour today?" he says.

But before I can answer, Mom comes out of our house, walks to her cruiser, and says, "Quinnie, would you please pick up the order for Ceil and Edgar and run it down there?—Good Morning, Dominic."

She doesn't wait for a response from either of us. She gets in her cruiser, backs out, and jackrabbits a little bit as she heads out of town, ready to capture crime on video.

"Wanna help me make a delivery?" I ask Dominic.

"Sure. But I have to eat something. My mom says she set up an account for me at the café, so I can eat whatever I want, whenever I want. I suppose that's kind of like you."

"I guess." I don't usually think about it. I eat when I'm hungry. I never pay for food at Gusty's. It's like my personal free restaurant. "Okay, let's go eat something and take the delivery to Ella's house, and then we can talk about something."

"What?" Dominic asks.

"First things first."

Edgar and Ceil's takeout package is ready when we get to the café, and Dad is eager for us to get it down there.

I whine a little bit. "Can we eat first?"

"Got you covered," Dad says. He puts a small brown bag on the counter for each of us. "Fried-egg-and-crab-cake breakfast sandwiches with blueberry muffins." He leans under the counter, comes up with a handful of paper napkins, and stuffs a few in each bag.

Then he swings a big coffee thermos up onto the counter. It's the size of a gallon of milk and has a handle at the top and a spigot on the side.

"That's new," I say.

"Yep. Jack Philpotts dropped it off. He brought two. We'll have them in rotation. Tell them it's as mind-crushing as I can get it."

Dad looks pleased with the whole situation, which is good to see. Not only is he happy about all the orders, he's getting into the challenge of a stronger cup of coffee. "Now, go, please. While it's nice and hot."

Dominic reaches for the thermos and his breakfast bag. I grab the takeout order and my own bag. As we walk across the parking lot, I look up for Buster and the seagull gang because I have some biscuit crumbs for them, but they're not around. I figure they got into some fish heads by the lobster pound.

Dominic holds his breakfast bag up to his nose. "Oh, man, this smells so good. Can't we just stop and eat it?"

"You heard our orders. Deliver the food while it's hot."

"I'd like to deliver this blueberry muffin into my stomach right now."

"Dad usually cracks the top and smears some butter in it."

"*Ooh!* You're killing me."

A few cars go up and down Mile Stretch Road as we head to Ella's. From behind me, I hear the familiar *grrr* of Ms. Stillford's old Volvo. She stops next to us and powers down the window. "Lovely Saturday morning!"

I can't help myself. I have to report my progress. "Ms. Stillford, I read *Dracula*."

"Excellent, Quinnie. Quite different from *Transylvanian Drip*, isn't it?"

"Uh-huh." Oh great, I didn't mean to start a full-on school conversation. If I had wanted to, I'd have said, *Urgh, Ms. Stillford, why are you making us read things that are keeping me up at night imagining there are vampires in Maiden Rock!?*

"Well, I'm off to Three Kittens Yarn Shop in Rook River," Ms. Stillford says. "They have some new angora." She raises her eyebrows like new angora is something special. "See you two. Have a lovely day!"

We keep walking.

"I just want you to know," Dominic says, "my stomach hates you."

I laugh. "Fine, stuff your face with that blueberry muffin if you can't wait."

I'm kidding, but he's not. He pulls the muffin out and peels back the waxy brown paper. Drips of butter roll down his hand. Either he doesn't notice or he doesn't care. In one bite, a third of a big muffin disappears.

"Zats gud," he manages to say with his mouth stuffed. After a swallow, he smiles. "My stomach likes you again."

A few houses away from Ella's, something catches my eye. Buster and his buddies have gathered on Ella's roof. Several of the seagulls are perched on the ridge of the roof. Others are lazily circling above it. "Hey, Buster!" I call out to him. "Given up on Gusty's?" I look at Dominic. "Gulls are fickle things."

"That's scavengers for you," he says. "They go where the food is."

"I guess they figured out we were bringing it here."

Before we can knock on the door to Ella's house, Ella throws it open.

"Hi!" She grabs the delivery bag from me. "I'll

be right back." She turns and runs it into the kitchen, then returns for the coffee. "Right back." Once she's delivered the coffee, she comes out and shuts the door behind her. She looks unusually cheery. "What are we going to do this morning? Ben gets back from practice at two. He's going to meet me at Gusty's."

I guess we're not going to see her aunt and uncle today. "How are Edgar and Ceil?" I ask.

"They are great." Ella is bubbly. "They got a great night's sleep. They woke up looking better than I've seen them look in a long time."

"Oh, good." I still wish Dominic could meet them, but since Ella's steering us away from the house, I guess that won't happen.

I look back at the seagull convention. "Did you see all the gulls on your roof?"

"Did I see them? Those noisy squawkers woke me up this morning with all their screeching and cawing." She shivers and shakes her hands. She's changed her nails from Darling Daffy Gold to the dark red color that Ceil was wearing. "How do you get rid of them?"

"I recommend not bringing large quantities of lobster fries into the house," Dominic says. This draws a look from Ella, which he immediately picks up on. "No, I mean, they like the fries. Hot fat, that's all."

Ella relaxes. "You may be right. We've brought more food into the house in the last day or so than we usually eat in a week, and it all smells so good."

"Where are you throwing the trash?" I ask. "They love to pick in the trash bins."

"Oh, yeah. That must be it."

"So, I think we should take Dominic over to the nature center," I tell Ella.

Ella looks surprised. "Why?"

"Because last night we think we saw a wolf out on the rocks," I say.

"It could have been a German shepherd," Dominic adds.

"Oh, no!" Ella whips around and grabs my arm. "When? Ceil and Edgar were walking on the beach last night. Scary!"

"Calm. Calm," I say. "Ceil and Edgar were fine this morning, right?"

She takes a breath and laughs. "Yeah. But I'm going to have to tell them not to take night walks if you really saw a wolf. What time was it?"

Dominic and I look at each other like, *err.*

"Pretty late," I say. "It was dark. Anyway, that's why we want to go to the nature center. Mom says Ben's uncle will know if there are wolves around here."

"Okay." Ella is completely on board for this. "Oh, and the trash. I have to remember to tell them about not putting food in the trash bins." She taps out a note on her phone. "Don't put food in the trash bins. Gulls get into it."

Gulls and who knows what else.

9

After the fifteen-minute walk from Ella's place, Ella, Dominic, and I turn onto the rutted sand driveway that leads to the nature center. Soon we're hemmed in by the woods, and the pine and balsam branches overhead make it as dark as late evening. The walk sends my mind tumbling back to Jonathan's trip to the castle. I shiver and pick up my step. Once we reach the clearing, the farmhouse comes into view. A small sign hanging from the porch railing says *Becker's Wood Nature Center*.

"Hey. What's up, kids?"

John Denby steps through the nature center's front door, wiping his hands on a rag like he's cleaning off motor oil.

"We've come to ask about wolves," I say. "My mom said you'd know."

"What do you want to know about wolves?" John Denby asks.

I realize that Dominic is about to talk and I haven't introduced him. "Oh, and this is Dominic—" I start, but John Denby is more interested in the wolf topic.

"You know, you're the second folks to ask me that today." He waves us onto the porch. "Sister Ethel called about it this morning."

*Sister Ethel?*

"They lost one of the cats last night to an attack. She thought it might have been a dog, but it was pretty messy."

"Oh, no!" My chest knots up. "Sister Rosie must be sick about it."

"I guess she's pretty tore up. Cat had a name and everything."

"Not Esmeralda!" Sister Rosie has loved Esmeralda so much she's never let the cat be adopted. "Please not Esmeralda."

"May have been, but I don't recall."

"So was it a wolf?" Ella asks. Her eyes are wide like saucers. I know she's calculating the distance from the cat rescue lighthouse to her house, just on the other side of the rocks.

"Did you see the cat? Esmeralda? I mean, how did it happen?" I ask.

Ella looks at me like I'm being a little creepy, but Dominic has a flicker of curiosity behind his eyes.

"I didn't see it myself," John Denby says, "but Sister Ethel said the throat was ripped."

I shudder. "Could a wolf do that?" I ask.

"No. No. Couldn't 'a' been. No wolves around here. Maybe a mad dog, but I haven't seen any sign of one. More 'an likely it's a starving coyote."

"Would a starving coyote do that?" I ask.

John Denby tips his head back and forth, weighing the possibility. "That's the thing . . . not usually. When it's a long, cold winter, they run outta food, get desperate, start coming into the settled areas. But they tend to eat their prey right up. Maybe leave the tail and the innards. I checked around, though. No other reports of coyotes taking domestic pets."

So that dog was no dog *or* coyote.

"Quinnie and Dominic saw it," Ella blurts.

John Denby cocks his head in surprise. "Where? And when?"

*Great.* So much for not getting outed for being on the beach in the middle of the night.

Dominic starts, "We were walking on the beach last night and saw what we thought was a dog, maybe the size of a German shepherd, on the rocks between the beach by Ella's house and Pidgin Beach."

Here it comes. "When was this?" John Denby asks. "That cat happened early this morning."

I know it's going to get right back to Mom, but my voice cracks it out anyway. "Maybe four a.m.?"

Ella looks at me with a sly smile. Dominic has somehow shrunk beneath his hat.

John Denby's eyebrows are up in his hairline. In true Maiden Rock old-guy form, he doesn't flip out, but he says the most threatening thing he can say. "Hmm." That means he'll take it up with my mom. "Ears pointy or roundish?"

What can I do? The truth is out. I'll have to explain myself to Mom. Worse than that, Dominic will go under her microscope. "We weren't close enough to see the ears."

"It was climbing the outcropping?"

"Yes, it went from the Maiden Rock side to the Pidgin Beach side."

"Could it have been a big cat? Cougar, maybe?"

Dominic somehow finds his voice. "Now that you mention it, the ears may have been a little roundish. I'm not sure."

"The cougar pups have more oval ears," John Denby says. "But a grown coyote looks a heck of a lot like a German shepherd."

I am losing interest in this conversation, since I'm full-blown fantasizing that the wolf turned back into

70

a vampire and sucked the cat's blood. "Well, thanks," I say. "We ought to go."

"Ayuh." That's all John Denby has for a good-bye.

Back out on the road, my stomach starts to churn. Sand is all up in my Vans, but I don't care.

"Hey!" Ella yells. "Is somebody going to tell me what you guys were doing on the beach at four in the morning?"

I walk on for a bit, wandering over onto the shoulder of the road. The vision of a vampire attacking poor Esmeralda is running through my brain. I don't want to say anything to Ella about it yet, but she's stopped us in the middle of the road, hands on her hips.

"I was reading *Dracula*, and I got scared, and I . . . I texted Dominic, and he said, 'Let's go for a walk' . . . and it seemed like a perfectly good idea—"

"Until we saw the . . . whatever," Dominic says.

"You guys are so busted," Ella says. Pretending to get hysterical, she adds, "OMG, you were out there with a starving coyote! You could have been killed."

"Okay, shut up," I say, then make the sign of the cross and point two fingers in her direction.

# 10

Dad comes home early, which is a really bad sign. I lean against the upstairs wall and strain to hear my parents' conversation in the kitchen. I'm not officially on lockdown yet, but I know it's coming.

Dad tells Mom that the sisters didn't come in for pie today because Sister Rosie was so upset. And then there's the talk about me.

"Four o'clock in the morning, Gus. What could she have been thinking?"

"I don't know, Margaret. Is it this Dominic? Where'd you say they were from?"

*Not good. Dad's calling him "This Dominic."*

"Were Ben and Ella out there too?"

"If they were, no one's talking," says Mom.

"Have you spoken with Dominic's parents?" Dad asks.

"Yes. They are as concerned as we are. These kids

shouldn't be out at all hours of the night, coyotes or no coyotes. It's just not safe."

"You're going to talk to Quinnie?"

"Oh, yes," Mom says.

There is nothing like listening to a jury discuss your fate. One thing I know is that my mom will take her time before she comes upstairs. She always plans out her lectures.

I text Dominic.

Me: *Have they done anything to you yet?*

Dominic: *They told me I was not allowed out of the house between the hours of ten pm and seven am.*

Me: *That's not so bad.*

Dominic: *They also said I embarrassed myself and them by endangering you on the beach.*

Me: *How could you have known we'd be in danger?*

Dominic: *I asked that.*

Me: *And?*

Dominic: *Bad question. My dad's face went bloodred. I guess I was supposed to know the answer.*

Me: *I don't think they'd be this crazy if there wasn't a coyote/wolf.*

Dominic: *If there wasn't a coyote/wolf, they'd never have known we were out there.*

At a knock on my door, I toss my phone under the covers. My theory is that if Mom doesn't see it,

73

she won't think to take it away as a punishment.

"Quinnette?"

I don't say anything because I know she's coming in anyway. I just sit on the bed and wait.

Mom enters with a familiar look on her face. Worry-wrinkles between her eyebrows. Jaw set in a determined position. She doesn't make eye contact.

"So." She looks out my window to the ocean before sitting down at my desk. She considers my papers, laptops, scrunchies, beach rocks, hairbrush— everything—like they're going to reveal something important. After flipping through the pages of *Transylvanian Drip,* she finally turns to me. "You heard about Esmeralda?"

My nose burns. Tears are coming. That means it was definitely Sister Rosie's favorite cat.

"That could have been you and Dominic. You could have had your throats ripped open."

Too graphic, Mom! I want to say, *How could I have known? It was just a walk! We're fine!* But she has a point. Coming face-to-face with a hungry coyote would've been bad. And a wolf, well, that would've been worse. And if that wolf were a vampire? Wait—what is my *Dracula*-drenched brain jumping to?

Mom says, "Stay off the beach. Until this coyote

is captured and I know the beach is safe, you're sticking close to home. The main road, Gusty's, and Ms. Stillford's."

I notice that Ella's house isn't on the list. Trouble is, that's exactly where I need to be if I'm going to learn more about vampires. I mean, there are two serious bloodsucking experts in that house at this very moment, and their knowledge might come in handy with this . . . this whatever-it-is on the loose. Besides, who will deliver the takeout orders?

"Give me your phone," she says.

*Groan.* I reach under my covers and pull it out. Her hand is waiting.

"I'll just keep this until tomorrow," Mom says. "And until I decide to give it back, there'll be no phoning, no texting, no emailing, no messaging—no contact with Dominic, Ben, or Ella."

*Whine.* I expected Dominic, but why Ella and Ben?

"You will stay home and think about the decision you made to sneak—don't even try to tell me you didn't sneak—out of the house in the middle of the night."

She turns my phone off in front of me, which I think is particularly harsh, and tucks it in her pocket before she walks over to kiss me on the head.

"I love you. I want you to grow up in one healthy, unscarred piece."

On her way out, she says, "I'm glad you told John Denby where and when you saw the coyote. That was the right thing to do," then quietly shuts the door.

My first reaction is to reach for my phone and text Ella—but forget that. And I *definitely* can't go to her place, which means no asking Edgar and Ceil about what they might've seen last night. Then it hits me that I should actually read my copy of *Transylvanian Drip*. It's basically the next-best thing.

At first, I have to practically read out loud to pay attention.

This is the story: Count Le Plasma is a seven-hundred-year-old guy vampire who travels all around the world going to fancy events, including international film festivals like Cannes and Sundance. He likes these places because they are crowded with beautiful people like actors and actresses. He especially likes the actresses at the premiers who have low-cut dresses with their necks exposed. Ella says that if you read all the Count Le Plasma books, you'll be able to guess which actresses–turned–bloodsucking vampires are thinly-disguised versions of real Hollywood stars.

Anyway. The Count has two helper vampire seductresses. They are gorgeous, of course. They're kind of knockoffs of Bram Stoker's beautiful vampiresses. They follow Count Le Plasma from one premier to another, and he lets them have the actors, since he only wants the actresses. The problem is, the actresses and the actors are getting so skinny that they don't supply enough blood for the Count or the helpers. So the Count makes a plan to rob the Red Cross Blood Bank in Park City, Utah, while everyone is busy with the Sundance Film Festival.

Count Le Plasma's grand scheme is to make the night guard at the blood bank let him in so he can pack up all the blood bags and beat it. Since the guard won't just do that voluntarily—it's his job to be a guard, after all—the Count decides to kidnap the guard's prize-winning Persian cat, Fidela. You guessed it: Le Plasma holds the cat hostage until the guard lets him into the rare-blood-type vault. I guess rare blood types are gourmet items for vampires. Okay.

At 9:20 p.m., I get up to go to the bathroom, and I'm laughing to myself. I really should have read this book more closely before. It's hilarious. And so ridiculous, it's believable.

I dive back in.

It turns out that being the Count's helper is a raw deal. Count Le Plasma makes the vampiresses do all the hard work. They have to snatch the cat and hold it hostage until he says they can let it go.

So the Count's assistants rent a windowless cargo van from U-Haul. These vampires may be like six hundred years old, but they never took a driving lesson or a driving test, so they drive like crazy people. I'm wondering what will happen if they get stopped by a patrolman. Uh-oh. They do. Oozing neck gore follows.

After that, the vampiresses—whose names are Treen and Vera, by the way—break into the guard's house while he's working at the blood bank. It's not much of a break-in. They have superhuman strength, so Treen flicks the locked door open with a stiletto fingernail. She and Vera find the fancy Fidela and stuff her in a carrying crate and cover it with a blanket. They're almost ready to leave the guard's house when Treen realizes that if they're going to keep the cat in the van for a few hours, they'd better bring along a poop box.

They didn't plan for that, so they have to scramble around the house for the pan and liners and litter.

They also didn't count on Fidela being such a whiny, complain-y thing, and they worry that the noise might make the neighbors suspect something, so they find a blue tarp in the garage and throw it over the crate.

Under instructions from Count Le Plasma, Treen and Vera park the van in a vacant lot about three blocks from the blood bank. After a couple of hours, Fidela's constant meowing convinces the assistants she wants food. So at midnight, Treen goes to the local convenience store to get Gourmet Tuna Delight Dinner for the mewing, annoying hairball of a cat. Unfortunately, Treen doesn't have cash or credit cards, so she's obliged to steal the cans.

When the clerks try to stop her . . . oh, the poor clerks. More oozing neck gore follows. I'm not sure exactly why they get in her way. Anybody that has ever seen a vampire movie should be able to recognize those fingernails, the white skin, the arched eyebrows, and those protruding incisors.

I admit it. I'm reading every word now. I'm totally into the story. I can hear the Transylvanian music. I have goosies all over my arms and the back of my neck. I cannot wait to find out what goes down with Fidela. But first, I have to find out more about the kind of weirdos who would write something like this—especially since they're hanging out a few houses away.

I turn to the back flap. There's no picture of the author, "Victoria Kensington," just this paragraph:

*Victoria Kensington is the author of sixteen bestselling Count Le Plasma novels. She has been voted the No. 1 horror writer for twenty years in a row by Horror Readers of America and has received the title Lady of Horror by the Vampire Society of England. She lives in London and is very private about her relationship with Count Le Plasma, who imparts to her the details of his life, which form the basis for her books.*

Who believes this? Do thousands of Victoria Kensington fans imagine that she actually knows a real vampire who tells her stories about his blood-sucking adventures? Am *I* one of those fans? Because right at this very moment, I'm kind of thinking that maybe *I do* believe it. Or I *could* believe it. I mean, I know Edgar and Ceil are Victoria Kensington. So, if *they* are the ones who talk to Count Le Plasma . . . well, that would explain why a wolf was near their house last night. And not just any wolf—a wolf who ripped the throat of a cat and drained its blood. A wolf who's really Count Le Plasma!

I am so tired. I have to go to sleep. I'm starting to hallucinate.

Is that a wolf howling? Yep, I'm definitely start-ing to hallucinate.

But I'm sure I hear a high-pitched yip-howl in the distance. And then some kind of fierce crack. Was that a gunshot?

# II

I sit up in bed Sunday morning with another head-ache, and now my bones ache too. Thinking too much about vampires really takes a lot out of you. Outside, rain's falling on a gray ocean, and no one is on the beach. Mom must have put out the word.

I vaguely remember hearing howling and a sharp crack in the middle of the night. I reach for my phone to text Ben. Oh, right—I'm in a communications prison. I groan and fall back onto my pillow. What exactly did Mom say? *No contact with Dominic, Ben, or Ella.* But there's no reason I can't do a little research on Edgar and Ceil.

I grab my tablet and start a search. *I* know that Edgar and Ceil write as Victoria Kensington, but does the rest of the world?

I search "Who wrote *Transylvanian Drip*," and the screen goes nuclear with 12,500,000-plus results.

One of the first is a YouTube link to "The couple behind the Vampire Count Le Plasma novels," a clip from *Celebrity Dish with Buddy Denton*, a daytime talk show.

The clip begins with the famous host addressing the audience: "We're here with Edgar and Ceil Waterman, who have just revealed that they write the wildly best-selling Count Le Plasma vampire series under the name Victoria Kensington."

The audience claps up a frenzy. Edgar and Ceil maintain severe expressions.

Buddy: "So why now? Why reveal that you are the people behind the stories, after sixteen books?"

Edgar: "Frankly, Buddy, fans were already beginning to figure it out. We don't intend to change the name on the books, but, well, our readers were clamoring to meet us."

Buddy: "So it's a publicity thing?"

The audience laughs.

Buddy: "I'm kidding. But doesn't this present a problem for you? I mean—" (Buddy holds up *Transylvanian Drip*) "—this says Victoria Kensington talks to Count Le Plasma, right? And now we know she doesn't exist."

Ceil: "And? Your point is?"

Buddy: "So that neat little fiction is, well, gone."

Ceil: "Not at all."

Buddy: "I'm sorry?"

Edgar: "The Count still relays his adventures to us."

Buddy: "Okay. I'll play along. So you still get the plots directly from the vampire's mouth." (He gives the audience a big wink.)

Ceil and Edgar don't break character. They are doing a great job of acting—if they are acting.

Ceil: "I don't see what the difficulty is, Buddy. The only thing that has changed is the fans now know the real, flesh-and-blood people who are receiving the stories from the Count."

Edgar: "The stories are his. We simply tell them."

The camera zooms in on Buddy rolling his eyes, and the audience laughs.

Buddy: "Well, folks. You heard it here first. Edgar and Ceil Waterman, authors of the Count Le Plasma series, talk to vampires."

Music swells, and the YouTube clip cuts off abruptly.

I flop onto my bed and look at the cracks in my ceiling.

I hate to admit it, but the clip reminds me of something Ella told me about from one of her dad's books. His famous detective character, Monroe

Spalding, always says, "The cleverest lie is the one that's closest to the truth." Really, it's the perfect cover-up.

And this is what scares me now: if Edgar and Ceil really are meeting with a vampire, they won't have to deny it. I could tell Mom, and they'd say, *Yes indeed, we are!* And she'd laugh and say, *That's great marketing.*

But if the worst is true, that's not cool or funny or great marketing. It's a danger to all the cats and people at Pidgin Beach and Maiden Rock.

* * *

The morning drags on, and I worry over Ella's safety in that house. How can I tell her that her favorite aunt and uncle might be meeting with a real bloodsucking vampire? I can guess how that would go.

I hear a knock at my door, and Mom sticks her head in. "Coming down for lunch?"

Wow. Lunch. What time is it? "In a little bit. I'll maybe get a sandwich."

"You okay?"

Am I okay? No, I am not okay. Vampires could be roaming the beach. "Yeah."

"Love you," she says.

"Uh-huh."

"That's good enough for now," she says and shuts the door.

I turn on my lamp and push some of the mess of paper around my desk. I'm fidgety. I'm cranky. I'm going bonkers. It must be phone withdrawal. And I can't just say to Ella: "Edgar and Ceil are on the dark side." She'll hate me. I need to talk to Dominic.

Hunger draws me downstairs to the kitchen. The clock on the microwave says 2:20 p.m. The house is quiet. Of course it is. Dad's at the café. Mom's holding an open house at #4 Mile Stretch Road. But— yay, Mom! She's made me a peanut butter-and-jelly sandwich, and next to it is my phone! Thank you, thank you, Mom.

I'm chewing big bites of my sandwich while I find Dominic's number and press Call.

Instead of hello, he says, "You're sprung?"

"I am, and we need to talk."

"Meet on the beach?"

"Ha-ha. That must be a joke. I'm not allowed on the beach." Is he?

"At all?"

"Not until the mystery of the coyote is solved."

"That could take a while," he says.

"I know."

"Because it's not a coyote."

"*I know!*" Thank goodness, Dominic sees it too. "We have to do something."

"What do you mean?" Dominic asks.

"Would I sound crazy if I said that, just maybe . . . that wolf, from the other night? It might be Count Le Plasma, here to visit Edgar and Ceil. That's what I mean. What did you mean?"

"Whoa, I think your positronic subcompact unit is on the fritz."

"What are you taking about?"

"Never mind," Dominic says. "You have my full attention. Explain, please." His voice sounds mechanical.

"What are you doing?"

"Watching *Star Trek: The Next Generation*," he says. "It's the 'Dark Page' episode. So bad. Lwaxana Troi has a mental breakdown. I can't help myself."

"Isn't that show thirty years old?" I ask. "And will you snap out of it to help me?"

"Yes, but it's great. And okay." His voice sounds normal again. "Let's hear it."

"I can walk to Gusty's. Can you walk to Gusty's?"

"Yep."

* * *

It's threatening rain as Dominic and I head toward Gusty's. Soupy clouds hang over the surface of the Maiden Rock Tidal Pool.

"Just listen, okay?" I say.

He nods. We walk almost shoulder to shoulder.

"On YouTube, I saw Edgar and Ceil on a talk show where they made a *huge* deal out of saying that they were the ones who wrote the books *and* they were the ones who talked to Count Le Plasma."

"Maybe they are *huge* into selling books."

"That's not listening."

Dominic pretends to lock his mouth.

"They are telling the world that they talk to a vampire, which the world does not, of course, believe, because it is so over the top. But what if that's a total cover-up for the fact that they *actually* talk to vampires?" I stop to take a breath. "And what if the Count went to see them in the form of a wolf, like Dracula does in *Dracula*, and after Count Le Plasma met with them on the beach, where Ella said they went for a walk, he stopped at the lighthouse and drank a cat?" I take another breath. "And the reason he was here was to tell them their next story?"

We keep walking.

"Well?"

Dominic hesitates. "My turn now?"

I nod.

"I think it was a wolf. Totally. I think the wolf killed the cat," Dominic says. "But—I think it has something to do with Edgar and Ceil too. Because, one: you never saw a wolf here before. And two: it showed up the day after Edgar and Ceil got here."

I'm nodding and nodding.

Dominic continues: "No one has disproved the existence of vampires, so it is possible Le Plasma exists and can turn into a wolf—and probably a bat and other nasty stuff—and talk to Edgar and Ceil."

I clap my hands. "Yes!"

"But that last part is kind of a problem. Because although no one has disproved that vampires exist, no one has proved it, either." He looks at me like, *right?* "And just because Edgar and Ceil say it's so, that isn't good enough, because they are weird, and it really does look like a publicity grab . . ."

We're just about to walk into Gusty's. I plant my feet and put my hands on my hips. "I agree. But I think we can prove it all by ourselves."

# 12

I groan as soon as I see the counter at Gusty's. Dominic does a double take. We are experiencing the first spring sighting of the exotic *Flatland Fish Catcher*.

Seated at the counter are a couple of paunchy guys dressed like they just came from Boston or Philly and didn't even take the tags off their brand-spanking-new fishermen's outfits. I can just see the salespeople at L.L.Bean laughing their plaid shirts off as these two drive away with new waterproof waders, gear pants with ten pockets, vests, hats with netting, tackle boxes, and fishnets. Sure, it's all authentic Mainah stuff, but on these guys, it looks like part of a comedy skit.

Dad is trying to keep a straight face while he explains the menu. John Denby comes in, takes one look at them, and veers off to a table. Mom is polite, but as she leaves, she gives me a look that says, *Oh, boy. Here we go.*

We hear the tourists say they're staying at Miss Wickham's B&B and want to "really experience Maine."

Mom and Dad have always told me to be kind to Maiden Rock visitors because they probably just don't know any better. I mean, true, these guys aren't hurting anybody, and they are helping the Maine economy, not to mention the Boyd family bank account. They're just hard to look at and painful to listen to.

"Can't wait to eat me a *lobstah*," says the big one, "and see a lighthouse."

"And a moose," the smaller one adds.

Ella and Ben are sitting at our usual table. It looks from the empty plates and balled-up napkins as if they've just finished eating.

Ella sees me and cries out, "You're free!"

I shoot Dominic a look that says, *Don't say anything to Ben or Ella about what we were just talking about*, and he shoots a look to me that says, *That's the last thing I'd do.*

We join them in watching the L.L.Bean guys like it's a sitcom.

The small guy turns to Dad and says, "Where's that cranky old geezer who gives directions by saying, 'You can't get they-yah from he-yah'? We want to ask him how to get to Boothbay Hah-bah."

The man busts out laughing, which gets a half-smile out of Dad.

Eventually, Dad walks up to our table with a familiar take-out bag and the trusty glug pail of coffee. Ella and Ben get up to leave.

"Gotta get this stuff home," she says. "Are you coming over?"

While Dad is still standing there, I look at him with imploring eyes. He knows that the new safety measures say Ella's house is out of bounds, but I can tell he's sympathetic. Ella looks at both of us, like *what?* Then Dad does a remarkable, never-before-seen-in-Maiden-Rock thing. He makes a big decision about me without calling Mom.

"If you are home before it starts to get dark," he says. "Maybe even a little before that."

I turn to Ella. "Sure, we'll come soon," I say, *we* meaning Dominic and me. Inside, I'm jumping for joy at the idea of doing some investigating around the Philpotts' place. Ben doesn't look overjoyed that I'm bringing Dominic with me, but he doesn't look ticked off either.

When I look back at Dad to say thank you, he's brushing it off, like I shouldn't worry, like *he's got this*. Then some loud laughter from the L.L.Bean guys attracts Dad's attention back to the café counter.

I notice a gear pack on the floor by their feet with a strap for a rifle. Thankfully, there's no gun in it, so the moose in Maine are safe.

But it reminds me of last night. I turn to Ben. "Hey, did you hear anything like a gun going off last night? Was that your uncle shooting at the . . ."—I stop and choose my word carefully—"coyote?"

Ben perks up. "Yeah, he was. Didn't get it, but there was a yelp, like he grazed it. I think he's going out again tonight."

"Come on," Ella says, hoisting up the coffee pail. "Let's get this home while it's hot." Then she turns to me and says, "Say good-bye to the L.L.Bean guys for us."

We all laugh a little bit, and they take off.

As soon as the door is shut behind them, Dominic says, "Now, Sherlock, I'm dying to hear how we're going to prove that Edgar and Ceil talk to vampires."

"You're an A/V geek, right?"

"Right."

"Well? We start by setting up a surveillance camera outside the Philpotts' house. Easy peasy, yes?"

Dominic's interest shoots so high I think his cap is going to fly off his head. "Absolutely. Easy peasy. I know exactly what we need to do."

It doesn't take us long to eat two Gusty burgers,

some lobster fries, and two pieces of blueberry pie. Setting up a surveillance operation takes fuel.

When we leave the café, Dad calls out, "Before it starts to get dark."

"Yes. Fine. Okay." I try to be really nice about it because Dad was super wonderful for saying I could go, but sometimes being so closely watched just makes me twitch.

"Okay," Dad says.

I can tell by the look on his face it's taking every ounce of restraint for him not to say, *Be good, be careful, stay safe.* I smile and wave. That helps both of us.

* * *

Dominic's room is . . . different.

Of course, the only other boy's room I've ever seen has been Ben's, and I haven't seen that in a while. But when I did, it had a computer, some books, posters of sports guys and rappers, a pile of running shoes, a mound of dirty socks, a wet towel hanging over the chair back, a stack of *Running* magazines, a soccer ball, a catcher's mitt, a half-made bed, and two packages of Oreo cookies.

Dominic's, on the other hand, is a cross between Best Buy and Toys"R"Us:

94

Tripods. Cameras. Cables. Books. Electric guitar. Comic books. Funko Pops. DVDs: *The Dark Knight*, *Man of Steel*, *Star Trek*, *Star Wars*, *Avengers*, *Ant-Man*. I'm about to stop reading titles when I see a shelf that interests me. *Zombieland*, *Evil Dead II*, *Blade II*, *The Wolfman*, *Abraham Lincoln: Vampire Hunter*.

"We should watch some of these," I say. "The vampire ones."

Dominic stops digging in a box of video stuff and walks to the DVD shelf. He runs his finger over one, two, three rows of titles until it rests on a particular movie, and he pulls it out.

"This is what we should watch," he says. "It's the only movie ever made from a Count Le Plasma book."

I put out my hands. "Give. Give."

The cover of the DVD looks like the covers of the books: dark red, black, and silver. Creamy white faces, piercing eyes, blood–dripping fangs. The title is *AB Positively Drained*, and the blurb on the back says: *Is Count Le Plasma's next victim the Highland Princess at the Edinburgh Renaissance Faire?*

"I'm ready," Dominic says.

I look up, and he's got a lumpy backpack over his shoulder with a telescoping tripod peeking out of the top. He's grinning from ear to ear. He really loves this stuff.

"We could take it along and watch it with them." I hold up the DVD and waggle my eyebrows. "They'll be sitting still for over an hour, and we can study them closely."

"Or I could set this up outside while you're inside watching the movie *and* them."

"That works."

* * *

When we get to Ella's house, Ben answers the door.

"Where's Ella?" I ask.

"She's . . . I don't know . . . around." Ben walks over to the big couch by the fireplace and flops down. He immediately picks up his phone and goes back to a game. "She'll be back in like a minute. She may be in the kitchen."

Darkness outweighs the light in the Philpotts' living room, even though it's two thirty in the afternoon. No lights are on, and the curtains are drawn.

I walk toward the kitchen, leaving Dominic with Ben. I hear Dominic ask Ben what he's playing.

The hallway's overhead light has been dialed way down. And over the framed mirror that hangs opposite the stairs, somebody has draped a bath towel. Maybe it's broken. Bummer. I love that mirror. Every time Ella and I walk down the steps, we stop and pose in it. But if it's broken, why not just take it down? I carefully lift the corner of the towel, and—nothing. The mirror's perfectly fine.

Someone shuts the tap off in the kitchen, and I push against the hallway door that swings into it. As it opens, I see Ella standing at the sink, wearing floppy rubber cleaning gloves. The sink is full of water, and her arms are plunged in it up to the elbows. A pair of scissors and pile of cut-up pillowcases rest on the counter next to her.

"Ha! What are you doing?"

"You wouldn't believe it," Ella says, hiking up the gloves that must be two sizes too big for her.

"What's with the pillowcases?"

"I'm cutting them into strips and bleaching them for Ceil's arm."

"What happened?"

"She fell on the rocks last night and got a pretty deep cut."

"Does she need stitches?"

"OMG, no way would she go to the hospital. Think of the people who'd bug her. There'd probably be paparazzi. No. This is what she wants. She says it's an old family remedy."

"Crazy."

"Times two. But whatever." Ella looks at the DVD in my hand. "What's that?"

"You are going to love me. Look at this." I hold up the cover and she reads it out loud.

"*AB Positively Drained: A Count Le Plasma Encounter.*" She jerks her hands out of the water and grabs for it.

"Bleach! Bleach!" I tell her.

She rinses and dries her hands before I give her the DVD case. "I didn't know about this. When was it made?"

"It's ancient. Like, before we were born. Hey, what's with the towel on the mirror?"

Ella turns to me with concern on her face. "Quinnie, Ceil is so run down and so . . . I don't know . . . exhausted. She thinks she looks awful and she doesn't want to see herself when she comes down the stairs."

I squint like I'm trying to comprehend this.

"Seriously," Ella says. "She refuses to have mirrors anywhere in the house—they're all covered."

# 13

Ella has returned from upstairs after delivering the damp bandages to Ceil. I've made microwave popcorn. Dominic and Ben have miraculously found something they have in common—some phone game—and are talking about tricks for higher scores on Level 121. The DVD is cued up, and we are ready to start.

I look at Dominic like, *go set up the surveillance camera*, but he's sucked into his conversation with Ben.

Ella presses Start, and an organ begins to play the kind of music I imagined as I read *Dracula*. The room becomes completely still. The guys stop looking at their cell phones. All eyes are on the screen. I get chills all up in my shoulders. The scene is a raging storm in a mountain village.

The sky moves in dark blue waves, dropping sheets of rain.

A steeple bell chimes in muted tones.

A glass window shatters.

The music spikes to ear-piercing volume.

I squirm in my seat.

And when Ceil appears in the doorway, dressed in a black robe with a hood, I nearly have a heart attack.

"Aunt Ceil!" Ella says. "Look what Quinnie brought! Come watch it with us."

Ella nearly pushes me off the couch making room for Ceil, who glides across the carpet and slips neatly between us. I look at each of her arms for signs of injury and see, inside her left sleeve, above her thin wrist, the wrapped strips of white cotton.

Ben grunts and picks up his phone.

Dominic says, "I gotta call my parents. I'll be back," and quietly grabs his backpack and ducks out the front door.

*Good. He's on the job.*

Ella, Ceil, and I keep our eyes riveted to the screen until the film's end. It's scary, and a little funny, but it jangles my nerves raw. At least three times during the movie, I notice Ceil put a glass of water to her lips. She barely takes a sip.

Ella is right. Ceil looks terrible.

Ben stands up and stretches. "Gotta go."

As the credits roll, Dominic comes back in and says, "Oh, no, it's over! I guess I missed it."

I look at him and he smiles.

*He did it.*

Ceil disappears upstairs, saying she needs to rest.

On the front porch, we wave to Ben, who takes off on the path through the marsh, toward the nature center. Afterward, Dominic tells Ella, "Hey, when I was outside calling my parents, I noticed the gulls got into your trash. Want me to pick it up?" And she distractedly says, "Yeah, sure, thanks."

When she and I are alone, she wrings her hands. "I'm so scared, Q. She looked so good yesterday morning. Now she's worse again. I told her to stay off the beach at night, but she won't. She says it's the only fresh air she gets."

Ella's worried about Ceil, but I'm worried about Ella—and her dad—being in this house. If I tell her my suspicions, she'll tell me to stop kidding around. If I tell her I'm serious, she'll just get mad. I don't know what to say, so I don't say anything. I just give her a hug and watch her worry her way back into the house.

* * *

Behind the Philpotts' garage, I find bins tipped over and rolled helter-skelter. Dominic's picking up trash while Buster and his gang are circling above us. I yell, "Freeze!"

Dominic clutches his chest. "Jeez! Give me a coronary or something!"

"Where have you stepped?" I demand to know.

"Where the trash is, duh!"

"Back up, carefully. Step away from the bins," I say. If there's a chance a vampire-wolf made this mess and not a gang of gulls, we should be searching for evidence.

"Okay." Dominic steps backward, looking behind himself as if he's searching for the shoe prints he left on the way in. When he reaches me, he says, "What now?"

"We have to study the area for prints—wolf prints, coyote prints, people prints."

"Good idea," he says.

We crouch down and circle the area.

"There," Dominic points. "And there . . . and there . . . and there."

It's true. There are paw prints everywhere, as well as shoe prints. I take off my shoe and compare its sole to some of the prints. They're narrower and longer. They could be Ella's or they could be Ceil's.

Very few of the prints are man-sized.

"Pictures," I tell Dominic as I pull out my phone.

We both start taking pics.

When we're done, I ask him where he put the video cam. He's hidden it in the brush so it can pick up the path between the house and the dune above beach, including the trash area.

"Great job," I say.

"It's getting close to five," he reminds me. "Are you hungry?"

"Not really, are you?"

"I can pretty much always eat, and there are things at Gusty's I haven't tried yet."

"What about your parents? Don't you have to cook dinner for them?"

"Not tonight." He holds up his phone to show a text. "They're meeting me at Gusty's."

"I suppose I can drink a Moxie and tell you what you missed while the movie was on."

* * *

When I open the café door, Clooney Wickham is directing people to and from tables like a traf-fic cop, waving a coffeepot in her left hand and a plate of rolls in her right. According to Dad, she walked in one day about twenty years ago and went to work without really asking. She's got her own version of a uniform: T-shirt, cargo pants, and a baseball cap.

As soon as Clooney sees us, she walks over to my usual table and hurries the slow eaters along. I spot Mom at the counter, drinking coffee and talking to Ms. Stillford. Owen Loney idles on a stool next to them, sitting like a lump, cradling a mug with his rough lobsterman hands. He's not one for women-talk.

I'm barely in my seat when the Moldartos walk through the door, wave to Dominic, and then step up to the counter by Mom.

"Oh, man, the L.L.Bean boys are here," Dominic says. "I think the one guy still has a price tag on his vest hanging down under his arm."

Something I don't expect happens next. Clooney's face brightens when she sees the visitors, and she waves them out of the line to a table where people are getting up to leave. "Here you go, fellas!"

"John. Bob," my dad calls out and gives them a friendly nod.

"I guess their names are John and Bob," I say.

"How original," says Dominic.

John and Bob settle into the table like they've been coming here for thirty years instead of since this morning.

Clooney's soon back at our table with a menu and a Moxie for me. She sees us staring at John and Bob. "Those boys are from Ohio. They're staying at the B&B for a fishing vacation."

She must notice my disapproving look. "They're not so bad. They own a chain of electronic cigarette stores. They're just a couple of guys who want to enjoy some Maine time."

This is too weird. If there's one person who turns her nose up at summer people, it's Clooney Wickham of Auburn, Maine. She is a Mainah snob through and through. I look again at the L.L.Bean boys. They're pouring over the menu like they plan to order every item. And *whoa*, one of them—John or Bob—even waves Owen Loney over to their table. And *whoa*, Owen Loney gets up and walks over to them. And *whoa on whoa*, he sits down. I know Owen Loney shuns women-talk, but hanging out with the L.L.Bean boys? Really?

The world of Maiden Rock is off its axis. I look again, and Mom and Ms. Stillford have grabbed seats with John and Bob too. But I have new respect for Dominic's parents—they've stayed at the counter.

While Dominic looks at the menu, I sip Moxie. I tell him about Ceil's strange bandaging. About her distaste for water. We start to wonder about other examples of vampire-friendly behavior, but what is there to say? It's pretty consistent. If you were best friends forever with a vampire, these would not be strange things to do. What's strange is being best friends forever with a vampire.

# 14

At eight thirty that night, twelve hours before I have to face a compare-and-contrast exercise at Ms. Stillford's, it occurs to me that once again, I missed big passages during my first reading of *Transylvanian Drip*. Such as: I really sped through the big crisis scene. So I decide to go back to the part where Count Le Plasma's assistants, Treen and Vera, are in the van with the kidnapped cat. I flip until I find it.

Treen yanks open the van door and finds Vera with her fangs out, just about to puncture Fidela's neck.

"Vera! Stop!" Treen screams.

Vera looks dazed, like she's in a blood frenzy. Treen jumps in the van and pulls the door shut behind her. In a split second, she grabs Fidela from Vera's quivering clutches. But that ungrateful Fidela does not realize she's being saved. She bares her claws and starts slashing Treen's milk-white arms and face, drawing thin lines of bright red blood. Vera's gaze moves to Treen's oozing wounds, and before long, there is an all-out vampire fight with a spoiled Persian in the mix. Scratches and bites everywhere, cat fur flying.

If anyone had been standing outside the van while this was going on, they would have thought the Devil himself was courting a bobcat.

Even though I know that the cat survives, the story sucks me back in. It's chilly outside my window, and I want to get up and close it, but there's no time. I turn the page.

Treen and Vera are in rough shape after their altercation with Fidela. They're covered in bloody scratches, and the cat is licking her paws. Next, Treen complains about how long the Count's heist is taking. It's been almost four hours, and Count Le Plasma hasn't called to say he's got the blood.

An hour after that, he sends them a text: *There've been some complications. Stay with the cat. DO NOT LEAVE THE VAN*, he orders.

They wait. They glare at Fidela; she glares at them. It's a standoff inside the confined space. Then Fidela decides to use the litter box.

Being part animal, Treen and Vera have super sharp senses of smell. The fresh and juicy litter box contents have them gagging and desperate for the cool night air. But they dutifully do not leave the van.

A few more hours pass. The Count's helpers feel feverish. Their scratches are inflamed. The Count has stopped answering their texts. The litter box mound is growing.

Treen decides to leave the van and go to the blood bank to find out what's going on. When she gets there, it's locked up and dark. Crime scene tape is X'ed across the door.

So she goes to the guard's house. He's sitting in his living room, clutching a stuffed mouse toy, weeping like a fool, and muttering, "But I did what he wanted."

It all comes together for Treen. They've been double-crossed by the Count. They're left holding the cat, and he's absconded with the blood.

It's now the middle of the night, and the house is quiet. My mind is ticking through the events that add up to Maiden Rock's very own vampire story: our quiet town is visited by Edgar and Ceil, two writers who *claim* to talk to vampires and who slink around like ghastly creatures of the night. Wolves begin to howl mournfully, a cat meets its maker in a suspicious way. And if Edgar and Ceil aren't lying and Count Le

Plasma came here in wolf form to talk to them, then vampires might be . . . I stop. I don't want to think it.

I try to force myself to sleep. I squeeze my eyes shut. But the cat corpse mars my vision. If vampires are *real*, I want to cry. None of us are safe from having our blood sucked, and this is a much scarier life than my parents ever told me. The last thing in my mind before I fall asleep is a vision of Count Le Plasma telling Ceil and Edgar about how he pulled off the blood bank heist, while the two of them take frantic notes. And no matter who I tell about it, Edgar and Ceil will just agree with me, which will only make me look ridiculous.

We really need proof to show up on that video.

* * *

At six thirty in the morning, I get up and go through the motions of getting dressed. I brush my teeth like a robot. It's threatening rain again, so I grab a slicker and wait with my worries in the silent house.

At seven ten, Ella knocks on my door, and a minute later, we knock on Dominic's. By seven twenty, we are walking into Gusty's to pick up the three egg sandwiches that Dad has ready for us. He also gives us a warm cinnamon bun for Ms. Stillford, wrapped in wax paper and tucked in a brown paper bag. Dominic gives Dad hound-dog eyes and gets a cinnamon bun of his own on the spot.

As we are leaving the café, Ben and his uncle John stop in to grab their breakfast before they leave for Rook River.

Ella says, "Wish you could come talk about vampires with us."

Ben smiles and ruffles her hair. "Yeah, way sorry to be missing that."

Ella slaps him on the arm playfully.

He and Dominic *hey* each other.

I wave.

And we are on our way to Ms. Stillford's.

At seven thirty, we reach the driveway at #1 Mile Stretch Road, where a woodsy lane winds down toward the beach.

"What's down there?" Dominic asks.

"The convent," I tell him. Ella and I shoot each other glances. We haven't been in Our Lady of the Tides since before it was shut down for renovation last fall. "It's a spiritual center now," is all I say.

And as if on cue, a speeding van roars up behind us. Dominic jumps into the weeds at the side of the road. Ella and I just turn and wait for the sisters to come to a full stop.

We may have become too trusting. The van looks like it's coming straight toward us, so we err on the side of caution and leap to join Dominic. The van skids to a halt, lurches sideways, and slams into the row of trash bins.

Both doors fly open and the sisters hop out. Their veils flap in the wind as they rush over to the bins, straighten them, stuff the spilled garbage back in, and dust off their hands like this happens every day.

When they turn to us, Sister Ethel rolls her eyes. "We're a little late for our once-a-month check-in at the convent."

Dominic's mouth is hanging open. That's understandable.

"Headed for Blythe's?" Sister Ethel asks.

"Right," answers Ella. Then, to Sister Rosie, Ella says, "I'm so sorry about Esmeralda."

Sister Rosie's face clouds up, and a fat tear spills down her cheek. "Me too," she says. It looks like real waterworks will start if she says anything more.

I go to give her a hug and get bonked with the stiff curve of her headpiece. She leans a little, and we get the hug done, but she squeezes me so tight I miss a breath.

"We're a little sad that you haven't been to visit us at the shelter this spring," Sister Ethel says. She looks at Sister Rosie. "Today would be good. Can you come and visit after your lesson?"

"We will, Sisters," Ella says.

Sister Rosie looks so miserable that it's hard for me to say anything other than, "Sure." But I add, "Let me ask my mom." I know for a fact that Mom would not want us riding with the sisters, but I also know she'd think it would be a good thing for us to help them out at the cat shelter.

Still, this means Dominic and I will have to wait to look at our surveillance video from last night. Then again, I realize it means we can investigate the attack on Esmeralda. "Maybe I can get my mom to drive us."

"Nonsense, your mother's too busy. We're happy to do it," says Sister Ethel. "We have a pregnant calico pickup in Winston this morning, a yellow tomcat drop-off in Porterstown right after lunch, then a quick stop at Walmart. We'll swing back and get you at three."

She's right about my mom being busy. Mom's already at the post office, sorting the mail for delivery for her postmaster job, and she has to review building permits today because she's the mayor. And then there's always her sheriff job. Plus, real estate buyers could need showings at any time. I guess my hesitation is taken as a yes.

"Done and done," says Sister Ethel. "And Ella, we'll have a few good tunes going at the lighthouse."

Ella gives Sister Ethel a thumbs-up, and they do their little ritual they started last fall. The two of them begin to sing: "Trouble hanging 'round me . . . knocking at my door."

Dominic pushes his hat brim up with his thumb and nods his head like he's grooving on the music. He is being so cool about this.

They keep singing. "I give up a little but, yeah, yeah . . . but you always want me more."

Honestly! In the middle of a vampire crisis, Ella and Sister Ethel are enjoying an Ella Marvell moment. It goes on for two songs before the sisters climb back into the van and peel down the convent drive. I wonder if I should explain about Sister Ethel and Ella having the common bond of being blues goddess Ella Marvell's biggest fans, but Ella takes the lead.

"My full name's Mariella. I started going by Ella—"

"Because of Ella Marvell."

"Exactly." Ella is impressed that Dominic is so on top of his blues facts.

When we reach Ms. Stillford's, I knock on the big wooden door and she swings it open. We all gasp.

"Whoa," I say.

"Ha!" Dominic says.

"Hahahahaha!" Ella is all giggles.

Ms. Stillford wears a long black cape and a wig of black and red tresses, and her face is powdered white. Plastic fangs protrude from behind her bloodred lips. "Vhelcome to my kazzle. Khum in. Khum in."

Dominic crosses himself and points two fingers at her. Ella gets her cross backward, but it's a good effort. A couple days ago, I would have thought this was hilarious, but now I'm uneasy that Ms. Stillford's making a joke of genuine vampire safety precautions. Dominic sees my reaction and winks at me like we should play along.

Ms. Stillford ushers us into the hallway and leads us to her dining room, where cotton spiderwebs droop from the corners and wine glasses wait on an ornate silver tray, filled with what looks like thick red tomato juice. At each place, there's a set of fangs. Eerie, off-key Bohemian music, like the kind in the movie, is playing. It's *too*, *too*, *too* much.

Without a word, we slip into our seats and don our fangs.

"Shall we begin?" Ms. Stillford drops the vampire accent. "Let's start with the reading experience. Did the books frighten you? Did they make your pulse race? Make you shiver?"

Ella shrugs. "Not really, because I know they're books, not real life."

Ms. Stillford turns to Dominic. "Nope. Not me."

"Come on, guys!" Ms. Stillford says. "This is good stuff. Doesn't anyone here believe in vampires?"

I start to think, *Is this a trick? Does Ms. Stillford know something?* "Were you scared?" I ask her.

"Sure. Especially by *Dracula*," she says. "The setting was believable and the descriptions were so palpable. I thought it generated reader empathy for Jonathan."

"But . . ." I try to continue without sounding crazy. "Do *you* believe in vampires?"

Ms. Stillford grins, pulls three clipped stacks of papers out from under a book, and passes one to each of us. The cover page says: *Bibliography: Rausch, Menzel.* Vampirism—The Clinical Analysis; *Baumburger, Marshall.* The Science Behind Vampirism; *Jasliska, Brian W.* Frantic Bites: Clinical Evaluation of Vampirism.

We all look up at her like, *What the . . . ?*

"I thought we might approach this from more than a literary perspective," Ms. Stillford says.

I leaf through the document, which is at least thirty pages of small print. When I look at Dominic, he's a goner—already nose-deep in it. I don't know whether to thank Ms. Stillford or cry. Will this be the proof that vampires really do exist?

"'While being well explored in the arts, the appearance of behavior that resembles vampirism has also been found in a series of clinical studies, in which it is associated with a series of other pathologies.'" Dominic is reading out loud to himself. "Oh, man, this is fantastic."

I flip through the pages until a gray-tone photograph jumps out at me. The caption reads: *Fig. B: Photograph of forensic bite mark from Ashville, North Carolina, Country Coroner's Office.*

"Is it like a real thing or a crazy-in-the-head thing?" I say without attempting to read any of it.

"Looks like someone got chomped either way," Dominic says.

There is no avoiding the crushing feeling in my chest.

Vampires can and do exist, and Le Plasma is one of them.

# 15

Ella, Dominic, and I leave Ms. Stillford's with a new assignment—choose a favorite passage from *Transylvanian Drip* to read aloud—but all I can think about is how I can prove that an honest-to-goodness vampire is visiting Edgar and Ceil. It's one thing to read about vampire case files. It's another to have one running loose in your town.

In the meantime, though, I have another mission. When we ran into Sister Rosie and Sister Ethel this morning, we didn't exactly say where we'd meet them later on, but I know I'm going to need somebody's approval to get in that van and I figure my best chance is Dad. We walk the way of Miss Wickham's B&B and Loney's Lobster Pound on our way back to Mile Stretch Road. The path takes us toward the Maiden Rock Yacht Club.

"Oh, no. There they are," Ella says.

John and Bob, in their L.L.Bean outfits, are headed toward the yacht club too. They're talking so intently, they don't realize we're behind them.

"I wonder when these guys are actually going to go fishing," Dominic says. "I mean, didn't they come here for a fishing trip?"

John and Bob veer toward the yacht club door, but instead of going through the door, they walk around the building.

"Duh, guys," Ella says, "you gotta go inside to rent a boat."

We pass the yacht club and head toward Gusty's. The pool is on our right, as is the T-shaped yacht club boat dock. John and Bob point at the various boats, still in a deep conversation.

"Those guys have no idea what they're doing," Ella says. "Even I know those are sailboats. You can't really fish from a sailboat. Right, Quinnie?"

"You can, but it's kind of complicated," I answer.

"The L.L.Bean boys don't look like they can handle any kind of complicated," Dominic says.

* * *

I'm relieved to see my mom's car is not parked outside Gusty's. That means I can ask Dad and only Dad about riding in the sisters' van. He was great about my going to Ella's yesterday. Mom will probably catch me, but the trip is worth the risk. I want to find out exactly what happened to Esmeralda, and the scene of the cat-crime might provide some proof that Count Le Plasma has been creeping around Maiden Rock.

"Hi, guys!" Dad calls out from behind the pastry case. "How was school today? Want a whoopie pie?"

Dominic looks a little confused.

"Do you *not* know what a whoopie pie is?" I ask.

"Correct. I do *not* know what a whoopie pie is," he says.

"Even *I* know what a whoopie pie is," Ella says. She lands on a stool at the counter and spins around. "Yes, please, and thank you!"

I direct Dominic to a stool, then tell him to sit down and get his mouth ready. Dad puts a whoopie pie on a plate in front of each of us. "Soft chocolate cookie, cream filling, soft chocolate cookie. Pick it up with two hands and . . . bite in!"

"It's the size of a sandwich," Dominic says. He holds the pie up and turns it over a couple of times, then takes a bite. As with all first timers, his eyes roll back in his head. He takes bigger and bigger bites until it's history. Two bites into his second whoopie pie, he manages to say, "These are sooo . . . good!"

"Mmm-hmm," Ella and I say with our mouths full.

Dad laughs. "I do love to watch a first whoopie pie experience."

"Dad." This seems like the perfect time.

"Quinnie."

"Dad, Dominic hasn't seen Pidgin Beach yet, and the sisters have invited us to come to the lighthouse this afternoon and help out a little, and they are stopping by to see if we want a ride, and—"

"Yes, you can go, but no, you can't ride with the sisters. I'll call Mom to give you a ride. She's in her office." He pulls his phone out of his pocket and walks toward the kitchen. I hear him telling Mom about our plans. He turns and smiles at me and gives me the thumbs-up.

"They're here," Ella says. She's looking out the window at the Gusty's parking lot, where the sisters' van has just skidded in.

Sister Rosie jumps out and charges through the door. "Gus!" she calls to Dad. "A blueberry pie and six whoopie pies to go, please." Then she says to me, "Are you guys ready?"

I don't want to tell her that my parents won't let me ride with her and Sister Ethel because they drive like maniacs. I'm struggling to come up with a better reason when Dad comes to my rescue. "Sister,

Margaret is on her way to drive them over. She's got some business in Pidgin Beach."

That's enough for Sister Rosie. The sisters are perfectly happy not to cross paths with Mom, given their long history of being way too lax about the law. "Well, I guess we'll just pay for our goodies and see you at the lighthouse, then." The portly woman grabs the goods fast and pays in a blink.

The sisters drive away from the café at about five miles an hour, clearly expecting to be seen by Mom. A few minutes later, Mom pulls in with her real estate SUV and powers down the window. "Somebody here call for a taxi?"

Sometimes Mom is all sheriff, and sometimes she's all mom. Right now she's all mom, with a great smile that uses her whole face. Knowing she's not going to give me a lecture about riding with the sisters takes the crimp out of my shoulders.

Ella and Dominic climb in the backseat, and I hop into the front. Mom turns to me, squeezes my hand, and says, "Thanks for asking."

I look to see if Dominic and Ella saw the hand squeeze. They didn't. I'm a little embarrassed that Mom's saying thanks when I was actually trying to evade her, but I settle into the ride out to the rocky little outcropping called Pidgin Beach. There are no pigeons there. Just a lot of seagulls . . . and a lot of cats. But not as many cats as there used to be—and I'm just hoping the number won't get smaller while Ceil and Edgar are in town.

* * *

Twenty minutes later, we've driven out to the main road, headed south a short bit, then looped all the way back to the ocean. We wind up at a point on the coast approximately fifty feet south of Ella's house. You have to drive to Pidgin Beach rather than walk because there's practically a mountain between it and Maiden Rock. The rocky coastline protrudes so far out into the ocean, and it's so craggy and treacherous, that you can't climb over it—unless you're a wolf. Or maybe the Count flew in as a bat and avoided the slippery coastline completely.

As we drive in, I notice how sad the little town of Pidgin Beach looks. Nothing like Maiden Rock, where there's a mayor to make sure standards are maintained. The Maiden Rock summerhouses take a beating from the storms in the winter and need serious fixing-up in the spring, which Mayor Boyd makes sure they get. But the sea and raging wind bash Pidgin Beach all year round, and no one seems to care.

"Yikes," Dominic says as he looks toward the ocean. Waves hit the coast twenty feet below him, over the edge of the road. "Where's the beach part of Pidgin Beach?"

"Not every beach is sandy," says Mom. "Some are just rocky stretches."

"Why do people live here?"

"Not many people do, and it's not a vacation spot, that's for sure." Mom turns right and tucks the SUV into the short parking space next to the sisters' van. "*This* crumbling lighthouse was the only reason Pidgin Beach was designated as a municipality. And the light isn't even working anymore." Mom seems to be talking to herself, but then points to the clock on the dashboard. "It's 3:50 now. I'll be back to get you guys at 5:45, while it's still light. How's that?"

"Good." I say. *Go. Go.* Suddenly I'm eager for her to get going so I can start investigating.

She backs out and inches forward, then stops and waves me over to the car. "Don't climb on the rocks. They're treacherous, not like our beach. And don't handle the cats," Mom says. "Many of these animals are diseased."

"Don't climb, don't slip, don't pet. We got it, Mom."

She laughs. "Remember: 5:45, honey. Right here."

Ella and Dominic are already halfway down the sandy path to the lighthouse. Dominic's craning his neck to take it all in. He has to hold his hat on. "Talk about the Hotel Transylvania," he says.

"I think it's the coolest thing ever," Ella says. She wore flip-flops, which means she has to be careful about her toes, which have a coat of her newest polish: Azure Meridian Blue.

The Pidgin Beach lighthouse is ancient. It's not as large or majestic as the Portland Head, but it has a sea-lashed charm. The stones have changed from gray to salt-washed white, and the whole thing leans towards the Atlantic like the Tower of Pisa—which is why it no longer has a light at the top. Nowadays, the Pidgin Beach Cat Rescue calls it home, but today you'd never know it, since we can't see or hear any cats. Every other time I've been here, cats wandered along the path, cats perched on the top points of boulders, cats lolled on any stretch of ground where the sun shined. This afternoon, there's not a feline in sight.

Dominic is the first one to the bottom of the path. He's picking up pebbles when the small door at the base of the lighthouse flings open. Sister Rosie presents a tray with three cups of apple cider, her signature welcome gift. Sometimes she changes it to cocoa.

"Come in, come in. Have some cider," she says. She tries to keep cats from sneaking out the door. "I'm keeping them all inside until this, you know, coyote business is over."

The interior of the lighthouse is dim and musty-smelling. To the left of the entrance is a hallway. To the right, a wooden stairway winds up and up.

"What's down the hall?" Dominic asks like he couldn't guess from the squalling.

"Oh, that is the indoor cat quarters and fixer-upper room," says Sister Rosie. "That's where they're all staying right now. Ordinarily we use it for bathing and grooming the sick ones."

"Are you a vet?" he asks.

"Goodness, no." Sister Rosie laughs. "Ethel is the scientific one. She took a vet tech course. And Doc Norton comes by regularly. Me? I just love 'em up."

"And you bake," I add.

"Oh, yes. I do love to bake. In fact, I've been feeling a rhubarb cake coming on."

I wonder how two women with a blueberry pie and six whoopie pies could need a rhubarb cake.

Sister Rosie leads us up the stairway at a slow pace, huffing and puffing and joking about being not as fit as she should be.

After a six-floor climb, we emerge into a large, bright room with a kitchenette, table, living room area, and bunk beds. Against the round wall stands a large table with a computer, a large monitor, and a printer grinding out a stack of blue papers. Sister Ethel is at the computer.

She doesn't turn around, but she waves and says, "Hi, kids."

We all say, "Hi."

"Who'd like to fold fliers?"

"Me." I jump at a task that does not involve touching the cats.

Sister Rosie walks to an open window and motions for Dominic and Ella to come look. "You can see the top of Ella's house from here, if you get up on your tippy toes and look over the rocks."

As soon as they get on their tippy toes and spot it for themselves, I'm over there too. Sure enough, you can see the house. And you can see lots of the beach too. It really wouldn't have been that hard for a vampire to get past those rocks. Heck, a bat could fly right in.

I walk over to Sister Ethel, who is fiddling with the sisters' rescue website.

"Placement. That's the real solution," she says. "Rehoming as quickly and efficiently as possible.

Check this out." The home page has a picture of the lighthouse and some distinguished-looking cats relaxing on the rocks. *Rescue, No-kill, Neuter, and Rehome. In God We Trust* scrolls across the bottom.

"Where did you find Esmeralda?" I ask quietly.

Sister Ethel's eyes dart to Sister Rosie, who is occupied with Dominic and Ella at the window. "Quinnie, you don't want to know."

"I do," I say. Then I quickly add, "For school. I'm studying it."

She hesitates, then says, "I opened the front door, and there she was. Left at our doorstep. Thank goodness Rosie didn't see her."

"I heard it was . . . messy." I can't think of another way to put it.

"Poor thing," Sister Ethel says. "I don't think she really suffered. It looked like a fast attack."

"Was there a lot of blood?" I ask.

"Not as much as you'd think."

# 16

I'm sitting in the front seat of Mom's SUV, holding a warm rhubarb cake in my lap. It smells soury sweet. Somehow, Sister Rosie managed to whip it up during the two hours we were at the lighthouse. On top of the aluminum foil that keeps me from getting sticky, Sister Rosie attached a photocopy of an ancient recipe card in curly handwriting that says, *Mary Ellen Vetter's Rhubarb Cake.*

When Sister Rosie handed the cake and recipe to me, I asked her who Mary Ellen Vetter was, and she told me she was her grandmother's next-door neighbor on the farm in Dayton, New Jersey, where she grew up.

Dominic's ears had perked up at that. "Dayton? I know where Dayton is. That used to be farmland?"

"Almost everything used to be farmland, dear," said Sister Rosie. "Our farm was one of the first farms to grow tomatoes for the Gephart's Soup Company."

"That's so cool," said Dominic. "I'll have to tell my parents that. They'll love it."

"I'll have to make them one of my tomato-soup chocolate cakes."

Eek. That brings the Dayton, New Jersey, talk to a halt. Fortunately, we made it to the car with only a rhubarb cake.

"Do you have any homework?" Mom asks us all.

"We have to pick a passage to read," I say.

"I'm picking the cat-in-the-van scene," says Ella.

"I'm going with the Count in the vault," Dominic says.

"How about you, Quinnie?" Mom asks.

I'm looking out the window, thinking about Esmeralda. "I don't know yet. The man getting his cat back is a happy part. Maybe the only happy part."

\* \* \*

It's seven in the evening, and I'm sitting at my bedroom window, watching as Dominic leaves his house and runs down the beach toward Ella's. He's going to retrieve the video camera and its evidence.

Shifting my gaze down the beach toward the

convent, I see the Morgans have arrived for the season. They're walking in the sand with their pant-legs rolled up, and their little grandchildren are spinning in circles around them. The scene surprises me, since I thought Mom told people to stay away from the beach. I want to yell, "Get in your house! There are vampires on the loose!"

Two more people walk down the beach from the direction of the convent. It's John and Bob, wearing the same gear and bouncing down the beach with fishing rods on their shoulders like a middle-aged Tom Sawyer and Huckleberry Finn. They stop near our house and put down their tackle boxes. What a couple of doofuses—they're going to try and fish in the surf with rowboat rods.

My phone buzzes—a text.

Dominic: *I've got it.*

Me: *Hurry.*

I turn back to watching John and Bob while I wait for Dominic.

Me: *Seriously hurry. You just missed seeing one of the L.L.Bean boys hook himself in the bee-hind trying to cast a fishing rod into the surf.*

As soon as I see Dominic's hat bobbing down the beach, I go downstairs and listen at Mom's office door. She's on the phone talking to someone about a cancellation fee. I listen until Mom gets her way and starts copying down a credit card number, then head for the kitchen, where Dad has the kettle on.

The smell of strong coffee hits me in the face. Dad's poised over a line of mugs, pouring boiling water into ten different individual filters.

I give him a hug. "What's this?"

"I'm cracking the coffee nut," he says. "I learn better this way . . . a cup at a time."

"Are you drinking all of this?"

"Just tasting."

"Good, because if you drank all of this you'd never be able to sleep ever again," I say.

It works. He pinches my cheek. He has a smile on his face. I realize he almost always has a smile on his face.

"Dad."

"Quinnie."

"Can I go over to Dominic's, even though it's darkish? To work on a school project for tomorrow?"

"Uh, I don't know. Did you ask Mom?"

"She's talking to a cancellation."

"Okay, but can you do it in one hour?"

I absolutely accept this condition. "Yes. One hour."

"All right. Git!"

In less than five minutes, I'm in Dominic's room,

pacing back and forth as he downloads the video to his computer so we can look at it on his big monitor. We don't talk. He clicks and clicks, and finally the screen jumps to life.

"I set it to start at 9:00 p.m. and stop at 8:00 a.m.," he says.

The screen is mostly dark, and our pupils take a few seconds to adjust. We can hear the ocean crashing on the shore. Clouds move across the screen, casting shadows and then letting moonlight shine through.

After about five minutes of nothing happening, I consider the time stamp in the bottom corner. We have eleven hours of video to watch in the next fifty-five minutes.

"Can you speed it up?" I ask him.

"I can fast-forward until we see something."

"Hurry. Do it."

Dark and light wash over the scene in rapid waves, with no one and nothing passing between the beach and the house. Until something flickers by the trash bins.

"Stop!" I say. "Go back, go slow."

Dominic backs up the video, and we lean in.

"It's just gulls," he says.

We watch gulls try and tip the bins for a minute.

"Go fast again," I say.

Minutes pass.

"*Stop!*" I say. "Back up."

From the left side of the screen, a dark figure, slightly hunched over, walks past the trash bins and out toward the beach.

"Can you slow it down?" I ask.

My heart is racing, and I can tell Dominic is excited too, because he tosses off his hat and adjusts his chair. He moves the cursor over the back arrow, which sends the video flying in reverse, then hits stop when the figure returns.

We look at each other and take deep breaths in unison.

"Ready?" he asks.

"Ready." I can feel my heart beating.

Dominic presses play, and we focus on the figure. "I'll go frame by frame," Dominic says. He clicks around until the video appears as a series of pictures at the bottom of the screen. He enlarges the first one, then toggles one picture at a time as the figure ticks through its movements.

On the sixth tick, I yell, "Stop! Look." I point to the left arm, which has swung forward. At the wrist is a white bandage. "That's Ceil."

"Okay," Dominic says, "Ceil is going for a walk on the beach."

"Speed it up to normal again," I say. "Turn up the sound."

We watch. We listen. There's wild thrashing of underbrush, and very soon, we hear some stray squeaking sounds.

After that comes silence, except for the wind and surf.

We wait and watch. Minutes go by with nothing happening.

"Speed it up, speed it up." I press on Dominic's shoulder.

The screen lurches forward. The time ticker in the corner moves from 11:00 p.m. to midnight to 1:00 a.m.—all the way to 4:00 a.m.—with no one, and nothing, crossing the screen. Then, once again, a figure appears on the right and walks from the beach back to the trash bins. Ceil. She lifts the lid and puts something in the bin, then disappears toward the house.

# 17

That night, I toss and turn. The air is sticky in my room. I get up and wash my face. It doesn't help. So I pick up my tablet and open *Dracula*.

Near the end, there's a part where a vampire appears to a lunatic in an asylum—as a rat, then as a spider—offering to make him immortal. It makes me realize how many forms vampires can take. Wolves and bats and spiders and rats—at a minimum. Wolves. Bats. Spiders. And rats!

Wait . . . we forgot to look in the trash bin! When Ceil came back, she threw something away! What was it? Oh, man. Why didn't I tell Dominic to check the trash before heading home? Dumb. Dumb. Dumb.

I know I can text him to go. He believes. He agrees. He'll sneak out.

Me: *We need to check the trash bin to see what Ceil threw away.*

Dominic: *Done and done.*

Me: *You checked?*

Dominic: *Buster and his buddies beat us to it.*

Me: *What was it?*

Dominic: *I think there's a need for a gull funeral.*

Me: *A dead gull?*

Dominic: *Dead. Picked over. Pecked and plucked.*

Me: *By other gulls?*

Dominic: *My dad says, don't be the unlucky chicken who trips in the coop.*

Me: *Birds.*

Dominic: *Birds. Brutal. Bloodthirsty.*

Me: *Blood?*

Dominic: *Now that you mention it, no blood . . .*

Eeew. Gross. Disgusting. I can't believe I have to cope with this. I feel like I need to breathe into a paper bag.

Suddenly, the situation becomes clear.

Me: *I'm wrong. I've been wrong all along.*

Dominic: *What do you mean? Ceil was out late at night. She totally could've been meeting with Count Le Plasma.*

Me: *No. She's wasn't. Ceil didn't meet with Count Le Plasma. Ceil IS Count Le Plasma.*

I search for breath. How could I not have noticed it right away? The clues were all there: the pitch-black hair, the white skin, the bloodred lips, the dark clothes, the creepy long nails, staying out of the light—the covered mirrors! Vampires' reflections don't show up in mirrors! The mirrors would give them away.

And the coincidences are just too coincidental:

The first night Edgar and Ceil go on the beach, a wolf appears and a cat is killed—ripped throat but no blood.

The next night, John Denby grazes a mysterious howling animal, and Ceil starts sporting an injury to her arm.

The third night, Ceil goes on the beach and then drops a seagull in the trash moments later. Another animal snack.

It doesn't matter that I'm a good detective, because no one is going to believe me. I can hear it now. If I say there are vampires in Maiden Rock, I'll hear: "Don't get so worked up, Quinnie." "No need for all the drama, Quinnie." "Settle down, Quinnette." If I say *Edgar and Ceil* are the vampires, the lid will come off this town . . . and Ella will never speak to me again.

Fine. I admit I have a little bit of a reputation for being excitable, especially when I think I'm on the trail of a mystery. But pardon me if I think it runs in the family. I mean, I didn't decide to have these instincts. They're hereditary. Like mother, like daughter. But accusing Edgar and Ceil Waterman of being vampires is not going to go down well with Sherriff Boyd, Mayor Boyd, Realtor Boyd, or Mom.

What I need is hard evidence. I need to have a video of Ceil the vampire actually attacking an animal. And the best way to get that is to follow her. There's almost no other way than surveillance: tailing and stakeouts.

I need to get close to the Watermans and watch their every move.

Of course, it would help if they didn't stay locked up in the house all the time. And it would help if I wasn't grounded from going out at night or going on the beach or going pretty much most places in town. Either I've got to break the rules, or Dominic is going to have to do a lot of the really hard and dangerous late-night stuff.

But in the meantime, I have to get ready for school tomorrow.

* * *

All day long at Ms. Stillford's, I'm distracted. I'm so focused on real threats, I've completely forgotten about Dracula. How will I get in a position to catch Edgar and Ceil at their dastardly deeds?

Ella is busy reading her favorite passages from *Transylvanian Drip*. Dominic keeps kicking me under the table, and when I look at him he gives me an encouraging smile. Ms. Stillford is talking about the handout she gave us, asking what we think about "the science of vampirism and the V5 virus."

I spontaneously yelp and startle myself. V5! Could Ella catch the V5 virus?

"Where's your mind, Quinnie?" Ms. Stillford says. "You're not with us today. Want to share?"

"Sorry. No. It's nothing. You're right, I'm drifty."

Ms. Stillford, wonderful teacher that she is, saves me. "Some times are like that, Quinnie. Join us when you're ready. But try and hang in there a little longer. Eighth grade is almost over. Just one more day after this."

\* \* \*

The next to last day of school should be a big deal. I should be thinking about celebrating, but I'm torn between wanting to run home and taking Dominic aside so we can make our surveillance plans. My anxiety level reaches the stratosphere once I realize

Ella could be turned into a vampire. I'd been telling myself that Ceil and Edgar wouldn't bite her neck, but what if they have that vampire virus? Could she catch it if they sneeze around her? Still, I take one look at Dominic and Ella as we leave Ms. Stillford's, and I know it's no use trying to do anything until we've hit Gusty's for an after-school snack.

It's three thirty when the three of us slam into the café. Dominic wants two whoopie pies, and Ella is desperate to try an espresso from Dad's fancy new machine. Dad's placed it so customers can see its copper-lever beauty behind the counter when they walk in. It's a little overwhelming, actually.

"Hi, Dad. Is that it?"

"This is it," he mutters. Packing material is scattered everywhere, and an instruction manual is unfolded into a map-size sheet on the counter.

I slide onto a stool and spin the instruction map around. Then I turn it a few times and flip it over. "This isn't in English."

"Oh, yeah. There's a small little box with the English how-to's, but you need a darn magnifying glass to read it," Dad grumbles.

Dominic and Ella have lined up on the counter seats next to me, watching Dad try and figure out the Espresso Milano.

"Quinnie, go ahead and get snacks. I'm busy here," he says.

It doesn't take me a minute to slip around the counter and grab two whoopie pies.

"Ella? I don't think the espresso is going to be ready soon. Want coffee from the pot?" I look toward the good old round-like-a-ball glass coffeepot.

"Sure," she says. She's fixated on watching Dad. "Do you want any help, Mr. Boyd?"

"Nope. Nope. I got this. It just takes a little concentration."

I pour water in glasses and slide them across the counter, then resume my front row seat. I fidget while Ella and Dominic loll over their food and coffee.

Before long, Ben arrives with his uncle John. Ben sits down with the rest of us kids, and his uncle walks behind the counter to stick his nose in the mechanical confusion. He picks up the instruction map, turns it over a few times, and tosses it down by the napkin holder.

A few minutes later, Owen Loney comes in. He's instantly drawn into the scene. Now multiple men in T-shirts and cargo pants are blocking the espresso maker, scratching their heads and saying things like "that's one savage coffee machine" and "hard tellin'."

There's one whoopie pie left on Dominic's plate when the café door opens. Ms. Stillford is carrying a large box of something that clinks and rattles. When she sets it on the counter and flips back the top, we see two sets of old-fashioned cafeteria glasses. She lines them up on the counter.

"Here you go, Gus. Tempered espresso glasses. The tall ones are for lattes. Washed and ready to go. Now, one latte, please . . . whenever you're ready."

* * *

An hour later, espresso is squirting and sputtering out of the copper contraption. Everyone has had one except Ben, who sticks to milk. My latte smells better than it tastes, but drinking something hot from a glass is a fun experience.

Dad's first espresso gave him a foamy mustache that he wiped away with the back of his hand. The second had him hopping around behind the counter. Now he's on his third, buzzing around the café with a tray of samples and getting applause all around.

It seems like a great afternoon for Gusty's. There is sunlight shining on the town for the first time in days, telling us that the world is warm and safe. All the grown-ups are focused on something new, something good, something they crave. If they only knew what was lurking at the end of the lane.

Dad hands Ella a big sack of food and gives Ben the giant thermos.

"Tell your dad," he says to Ella, "there's the real stuff in there. Fully-leaded depth charges."

"Where're you going?" John Denby calls to Ben from the counter. "Don't you have homework?"

I jump in before Ben can answer.

"I can take the thermos." I look over to Dad. "Can I take the thermos?"

"Okay. But be home by"—he looks at his watch—"six."

Ben looks bummed. "Yeah, I got homework."

Dominic says, "That sucks. I'll hang with you."

He stands next to Ben, digging his hands in his pocket, genuinely sympathizing. And instantly Dominic goes on my list of favorite people. I mean, how much more can you ask of a person than they help you hunt vampires *and* they're good to your friends?

# 18

After a too-brief stroll in the bright sunlight, my eyes adjust to the gloomy interior of Ella's house. We head straight for the kitchen. When I see Ceil, my heart skips a beat. Ella had mentioned on the way over that Ceil's health was getting worse, and if I didn't know the truth, I'd say Ella was right. She's sitting at the table, wearing dark glasses. She doesn't look milky white. She looks pale and gray. Her lips form a thin, colorless line.

"Hey, Aunt Ceil. We brought real espresso depth charges and lots of food."

Ceil doesn't seem to hear at first. Then she startles at the sound of the paper bag being unpacked. "Oh, good. Great."

Ella pours a cup for Ceil and puts it in front of her.

I say, "Hi." I shiver. I just said hello to a real vampire.

"Hi," says Ceil. "You guys home from school?"

"Uh-huh," Ella says. At the same time, she catches my eye and shakes her head in worry.

"That's good." Ceil takes a drink.

I immediately want to pull out my phone and google: *Do vampires drink coffee?* Did Dracula drink wine? I can't remember. Do vampires eat normal food at all? Who's eating all the food Dad's sending here?

No sooner do I wonder this than Mr. Philpotts and Edgar come into the kitchen, apparently led by their noses.

"This smells great." Ella's dad pulls out a lobster roll and some slaw. He hands Edgar a Gusty burger. "Ceil? There's chowder and a . . ." He reads Dad's handwriting on the side of a wrapped sandwich: "Vermont cheddar grilled cheese with pickle and mustard."

"You know, I'm just not hungry right now. Save the sandwich for me. I'll eat it later." She takes another sip of the depth charge. I want to think that she's just sick, not evil. She looks sick. She acts sick. But I don't know the difference been a sick human and a sick vampire. I'd sure like to see her eyes.

"Will do," Mr. Philpotts says and puts the chowder on his plate. "Well, I'm going back in my cave."

"Me too," says Edgar. "Getting some great writing done these last couple days."

My mouth starts moving before my brain has a chance to catch up. "Are you writing a new Le Plasma book?" I ask.

"Indeed." Edgar smiles at me, and his pointy white beard doesn't look so scary.

My motor mouth can't stop. "Did the Count come here to Maiden Rock to tell you the story?"

Edgar turns to Ceil. I'm pretty sure that if she didn't have those glasses on, her eyes would reveal something big.

"Ha. Ha. Hahahahahaha!" Ceil's sputtering laugh sounds like it might drift into a cry.

Then Edgar lets out a chuckle, and soon they are both laughing like limp puppets. Ella and I laugh along with them, neither of us knowing what's so funny.

"Sorry," Edgar says. "It's not you, Quinnie."

Ceil pulls her glasses off and shakes her head ever so slightly at Edgar as if to say, "Be careful."

"Yes, Quinnie," Edgar continues. "Yes. We got the new story from the Count."

Ella looks at me and says, "Not really. They make them up."

There's a moment of silence. Edgar and Ceil look

at each other as if they have no choice but to deny it. "No, Ella. We get them from the Count."

I never imagined Ella would get mad at them, but it looks like she's about to.

"No, really. For real. You make them up," she insists.

"We get them from the Count," Edgar says flatly. He turns to leave. "I've got to go back to my computer and get some work done."

"Aunt Ceil, stop it," Ella says. "Tell Quinnie the truth. Tell me the truth. You can trust us. Tell us you make them up."

"I wish I could, honey. But I can't." Then she gets up, fills her cup, and walks upstairs.

"That's not funny," Ella yells after her.

I'm not surprised. I figured all along this would happen. It's the perfect cover. The cleverest lie is the one that is closest to the truth.

Ella pulls me up the stairs to her room and closes the door.

"Errgh!" She flops onto her bed. "I don't know what's wrong with them. They're acting so weird."

I want to say, *Well, duh, they're vampires*, but I don't. I want so much to get Ella on my side. I take a chance. "Maybe they do talk to the Count."

"Stop it! It's not funny."

"I'm not being funny. I'm just asking. They said it."

"Don't be mean."

My tongue hurts from biting it. Finally I say, "Okay. I'm not being mean. I just think they are too, too different."

Ella bounces off the bed and looks out the window, toward Pidgin Beach. "I'm telling you, something is not right."

"Ella, I'm trying to agree with you."

"By saying they talk to vampires? How is that helping? That's just stupid."

That's it. She has to be told. For her own good.

"Listen to me." I pull her back down and make her sit next to me. "*I* didn't say it. *They* said it . . . and they've done a lot of other things too."

"I told you, they're from Brooklyn."

"This isn't about Brooklyn. It's about Edgar and Ceil Waterman—people you love."

Ella's shoulders drop.

"You have to admit, they *dress* like vampires. With all the black and the pale skin and the red lips and the creepy-ish fingernails."

Ella starts to object, but I give her an *aw-come-on* look.

"Fine."

"And they stay in the house in the dark during the day . . . and Ceil walks the beach at night . . . and there is the huge coincidence of Ceil on the beach and Esmeralda and the—"

"There was a wolf," Ella says. "You saw it."

"I saw a wolf at the same time that Ceil was on the beach. I didn't see Ceil."

She gets up and starts tossing things around her room like she's looking for a lost shoe. "There are no such things as vampires. No such thing as drinking blood. Nobody sleeps all day in dark rooms. Nobody sneaks out at night. Nobody turns into a wolf. Nobody kills Esmeralda."

"Ella—the next morning, Ceil looked wonderful, healthy, full of life."

Ella crumples to the floor in tears.

I run to her and hug her. "Ella, I hate to say this, but I think Ceil's a vampire, and probably Edgar too."

"It's not possible," she chokes out through her sobs.

"I'm so sorry."

When she lifts her face from her hands, her cheeks are smeared with Auvergne Mist eye shadow.

"This is crazy. I'm so afraid," she whispers.

"Me too. But don't worry," I say. "We'll do something. We'll take care of it."

"Take care of it!" Ella wails. "What are you saying? Do you want me to put a stake through Aunt Ceil's heart?"

"Ohmygosh, *no*! I didn't mean that!"

Ella wipes her face with her hands, making a bigger mess. "Well, what then?"

"I just meant we need to get evidence and show it to my mom, and she'll know what to do."

"What can she do?"

I don't know. What *will* she do? Arrest them for being vampires? Is that a crime? Just being a vampire? Arrest them for Esmeralda? "I don't know. I don't know if she'd even believe us."

"I'm not sure we should say anything."

"I know," I start, "but . . . what if you're not safe . . . or your dad?"

A sound comes out of Ella like a squeak and she starts crying again.

"Shhh." I pat her shoulder. "Let's go to my house."

Ella struggles up and trudges to the bathroom, where she washes her face and yanks a brush through her hair. When she comes back, she looks pale and thin and—with no eye makeup or lipstick—remarkably like Ceil.

As we walk downstairs, we pass Ella's dad's study. An intense conversation between Mr. Philpotts and

Edgar reaches us from behind the closed door. I hesitate and try to make out the words, but Ella pulls me forward, shaking her head like it's too risky to stand there listening. I ease my ear away from the door and run down the stairs after her.

# 19

I text Dominic to meet us at my house, and Ella texts Ben to do the same. We're a couple doors from home when the L.L.Bean boys' dusty green Honda passes us, going the other way. John and Bob smile and wave.

"Where are those guys headed?" Ella asks me.

"Heck if I know," I answer.

We stop and watch them cruise all the way down to the end of the road near Ella's house. They're moving like a snail.

"Must be looking at real estate," Ella says.

"Mom probably sent them on a house tour. Great."

"I don't know," Ella says. "They're not so bad."

I just groan.

* * *

We're a solemn gang of four, gathered on my back porch. I'm teetering on the porch rail, looking toward the beach. Ella's sitting in a faded blue Adirondack chair with her feet curled up under her. Ben's slouched in the comfortable wicker chair with his leg slung over the arm. Dominic was the last one here, so he's in the rattan chair with the pokey spring in the seat cushion.

"We need a plan," I say.

"What's the objective?" asks Ben.

"To find out, once and for all, if Ceil and Edgar are vampires," I say.

Ella pulls the neck of her hoodie up over her nose and whimpers.

"You can watch them all day and night, and you'll never prove it," says Ben.

"You can watch them all day and night, and you'll never prove they're not," says Dominic.

"If they go into the sun, maybe," Ben snaps. "Or you wave a crucifix in their faces."

"Whatever," I say. "One way or the other, we *are* going to watch them. All day and night."

"We need shifts," says Dominic.

"I can watch inside the house at night," Ella volunteers. "And text when they go out."

"I can be outside maybe every other night," says Dominic.

"I'll take the alternate nights," says Ben.

They all look at me.

"What? I'm grounded from dusk until dawn." I give it some thought. "But I'll watch my mother so no one posted outside gets caught. If she makes a move in your direction, I'll send a text. What should I text?"

"Text: *SOS*. For 'Sheriff on the Snoop,'" says Ella.

"If any of us gets in any trouble, like with, you know, vampires or anything," says Dominic, "text *MAYDAY*. And everybody better come running to help."

Ben gets up and stretches. "So when does this vampire chasing operation begin?"

"Tonight," I say. "Tonight at nine." I hold up my phone and we all check the time. "Take pictures."

"I'll have my D5500," says Dominic.

As they walk out the door, I hear Ben say to Dominic, "Whoa, you have a D5500?"

I hug Ella and tell her, "Text me constantly. Blow by blow."

* * *

By six a.m., Ella, Dominic, and I have been on the job for nine hours straight. Okay, I admit I slept from

155

one to four, but Mom was snoring away when I fell asleep and still sawing logs when I woke up. To my dismay, and a little bit to my relief, absolutely nothing had happened except for Dominic getting a lot of hilarious shots of the L.L. Bean boys trying to fish in the surf at about five a.m. I wanted to tell him to go out there and explain to those doofuses that they had the wrong rods—and real Mainahs would be digging for clams, not trying to fish—but he would have also had to explain why he was out near the coast at that time of the morning himself. Plus, he knows squat about fishing.

Anyway, the L.L.Bean boys must have been looking at real estate at the same time, because Dominic said they walked really slowly up the beach and back, pointing at houses—kind of like a couple of old aunties, looking at curtains in the windows.

At seven, Ella, Dominic, and I converge outside my house, then trudge up to the café for breakfast before we head to Ms. Stillford's. As we reach the parking lot, we spot Ella's dad. He arrived before his daughter, and he's loading his car with the coffee jugs and a bag of food.

"Have a good last day at school, kids," he says before he reaches into the bag and pulls out a blueberry muffin and takes a bite. "Ella, I told Gus to save you one of these. They are stupendous."

"Thanks, Dad." Ella sounds like the last thing she wants is a blueberry muffin.

We open the café door to a wave of great smells. As tired as I am, I know immediately that Dad is working the waffle iron, and I can already taste a buttermilk waffle, extra crispy, with Maine maple syrup.

He holds up the plate for me. "Morning, honey. Here's your favorite."

It is definitely my favorite. I sweep the plate out of his hand and take it to our table.

Dominic's night on the beach has him sniffing the air like a hungry hound. He waits at the counter while Dad stacks three waffles on a plate for him and smothers them with cranberry syrup.

We're chowing down on the waffles when Dad slides a dish of banana slices and fresh blueberries on our table. "Get some fruit on those waffles." A second later, he looks toward the door, waves to the people coming in, and says, "Morning, fellas."

I look up and groan. "They're here."

Dominic snickers. "They're everywhere."

"There's nothing to do in this town," says Ella. "Where else are they going to go?"

Mom comes in after them, and the guys wave to her excitedly. She slides into a seat next to them at the counter, and Dad pours coffee for all three. "I don't get it," I say to Dominic and Ella. "They're wearing the same clothes they've been wearing since the first day they got here. How gross is that?"

"Forget them," Ella says. "Concentrate on what we're going to do after school to solve our problem."

Dominic starts to explain to Ella how low light video works, but I'm only half listening. The rest of my attention is focused on the conversation at the counter. Mom is saying things like, "Real estate values are the lowest they've been in twenty years." And "taxes are the most favorable in the state." And "the Noonan place is a heck of a buy."

It's kind of a snooze until I hear the spongier L.L.Bean boy say, "I hear you have some celebrities in town."

I immediately tense up. I'm looking for Mom to do the same, but she doesn't. "It's been known to happen here in Maiden Rock."

"Oh, yeah?" says the skinnier L.L.Bean boy. "Who?"

I'm nearly off my chair, leaning to hear Mom's response. "I wish I could tell ya, Bob, but we respect our residents' privacy. That's one of the great things about living here."

Yay, Mom.

But Bob presses her. "That's a helluva good quality for a town. Still, I heard that those famous vampire writers might be vacationing around here. Any chance we can get an autograph?"

"Where'd you hear that?" Mom says.

"Oh, don't go getting mad at Miss Wickham. We were just walking down the stairs from our room, and we heard her talking to Blythe Stillford about it. They sure want to meet them. And, hey, we would too."

"You've read *Transylvanian Drip*?" Mom asks them. And John says, "Who hasn't?"

\* \* \*

All the way to Ms. Stillford's, I'm imagining Edgar plunging his fangs into the L.L.Bean boys' necks. *Shiver.* Those guys might be goofballs, but I still hope they don't get their blood sucked.

The last thing I want to do during our last lesson is talk about vampire novels, and I think Ms. Stillford senses it. Ella's turned cranky and answers all questions with one or two words. I think she's a little mad at Ms. Stillford for letting John and Bob know about Edgar and Ceil. I get it. They may be vampires, but they're *her* vampires.

At the end of the day, we give Ms. Stillford big hugs—even Ella—and then Ella and Dominic head to his house. I offer to stop at Gusty's and pick up whoopie pies, and before I'm two steps in the door, *ugh*. Déjà vu. The L.L.Bean boys are there stuffing their faces, with blueberry pie and espressos this time.

When I go up to the counter, the big one, John, says, "Hey, you live around here?"

I think, *Hellooo, I'm Gusty's daughter*, but I say, "Yes."

"You heard anything about those famous vampire writers visiting?"

"No," I say. And I try to make it look like I am giving it some thought. Inside, I'm thinking, *If you've got any sense at all, guys, you'll keep away from them.*

He shrugs, turns away, and opens his big trap for a forkful of pie.

When I get to Dominic's room, I tell them what L.L.Bean John asked me.

"He asked you about Aunt Ceil and Uncle Edgar?" Ella practically screams. "After what your mom told him! What did you say?"

"I said *no*, of course."

"Let's get down to business. We need to plan tonight's surveillance," says Dominic. His timing is perfect. Ben arrives a second later, and soon we're deep in conversation over camera placement.

## 20

Ben and Dominic decide they'll stake out Ella's house as a duo, in the event Ceil transforms herself into something extra-nasty, so they set out with Ella for her place. I leave Dominic's and head home.

Back at home, I walk past Mom's office door, and soon I'm worrying twice as hard about the guys' night watch. Mom's on the phone. I can't tell if it's the mayor's phone or the sheriff's phone. I know it's not the real estate lady's phone.

"The Pearly farm? Yes . . . the dog . . . mm-hmm. Oh, dear. Well, I'll go out there tomorrow morning, John. Can you get over there tonight and check it out? Right. We're going to have to get this thing sorted soon."

Oh, no! Ceil is at it again. I want to barge in and ask Mom what happened, but I don't need to. She opens the door and nearly knocks me over.

"Quinnie! What are you doing?"

"I was . . . I was . . ."

"You were listening?"

"I guess. The Pearly's dog?"

She walks into the kitchen with me on her heels. She's still wearing her sheriff's uniform, and the radio on her belt crackles static off and on. She turns down the volume.

"Gus, we may have had another coyote attack."

Dad stops at the dishwasher, mid-bend. "Where?"

"The Pearlys' black lab is missing." Mom pours a cup of coffee and slumps into a chair at the table.

"How long has it been gone?" I ask.

"Since last night. George let him out and heard a howl. The dog started barking his head off and ran."

Last night? Last night . . . Dominic was at Ella's all night with the camera, and he didn't see Ceil *or* Edgar slip out—unless he fell asleep, like I did.

"John Denby's going over there to look around and planning to go out again later," Mom says.

I want to shout, "It's Ceil Waterman!" But I bite my fingernail instead.

Mom looks weary and worried. "More summer people are arriving every day. Got to solve this thing." She's talking more to herself than to us. She gets up and walks back toward her office.

"Don't worry, Margaret. John Denby'll deal with it," Dad calls after her.

"He has to," she calls back.

Then Dad shivers a bit. "The Pearlys' lab was a good-size dog."

* * *

I'm beginning to think I should talk to Mom about Ceil and Edgar.

She is the law in Maiden Rock. It's her duty to protect us from dangerous elements. A debate rages as I get ready for bed: tell her they're vampires, which she will not believe, or *not* tell her and let her find out when I have two puncture wounds in my neck. I go back and forth with every swish of my toothbrush.

She has expressly ordered me not to harass Edgar and Ceil. That's one reason to tread lightly. And she has expressly told me not to get involved in an investigation of any kind, at any time, anymore. I have a dicey track record on this, but hey, I *did* find Ms. Stillford when she went missing. I mean, I figured out what was going on, and I helped capture the culprits.

Urgh! It's so hard to be a natural-born investigator and a powerless thirteen year old.

I decide it's all in the delivery.

I change from my pajamas back into clothes, to appear more serious, and head downstairs.

I find her in her office, searching the Internet for recent reports of missing pets.

"Mom?"

"You ready for bed, honey?"

"Can I ask you a question about investigations?"

She turns to me with an expression that says, *Okay, what are you up to?* "Sure. Go ahead."

Remember, I think, *delivery.* I try to come at the topic from an angle. "If you were trying to convince someone of something that is difficult to believe . . ."

"Yes."

"I mean, what if it's one of those things where if you believe it, you don't need proof, but if you don't believe, there's no amount of proof that will make you change your mind?"

Her eyebrows go unibrow. "Talk sense, Quinnie."

"I know you haven't met Edgar and Ceil yet, but . . . I just want to tell you a few things about them."

She leans back in her chair and the seat squeaks. "Go on."

"So, you know they have the superexpensive car?"

"You said that the other day. They must sell a lot of vampire books." I can see the real estate wheels in her head start turning.

"Mom." I want to snap my fingers in her face but, of course, I don't. "Did you read *Transylvanian Drip*?"

"Sure."

"So what kind of car did Count Le Plasma drive?"

Her neck reddens. "Well, I . . ."

Busted. She didn't read it either!

"I skimmed it," she admits. "Okay?"

I laugh. "I skimmed it the first time too." Good. I think this is going really well. "So, Mom."

"Quinn."

"They drive the same car their vampire drives."

"Honey, that's marketing. And they can afford it. So what?"

"Wait. Please." I prepare to tick down my list of evidence. "They dress in black from head to toe, they have super-white skin, they have bloodred lips, they have long pointy fingernails . . . Oh, oh, and they have tinted windows on their car, and they wear sunglasses to hide from the sun. They go on the beach at night, especially Ceil. And Ceil covered up all the mirrors in the house, she puts bleach on her skin, and she looked healthier the morning after what happened to Esmeralda."

I stop and wait for Mom to put the pieces together.

"And all these observations add up to . . . what?" she says. "Two New York writers are a little odd?"

They dress the part of writers of vampire books?"

"Maybe they're more than just that. Like, Ceil closed all the drapes at one thirty in the afternoon and went to bed."

I can tell Mom's irritation level is rising. "Sometimes adults take naps in the afternoon." Then something clicks in her head. "You're not trying to tell me you think they're vampires, are you?"

Everything in me says, *Back away from this conversation*, but do I? No. I don't, because the people of Maiden Rock could be at mortal risk. Including me. Including her.

"Yes, Mom."

She turns back to her instruction papers. "Okay, that was fun. Now get to bed."

"You have to stop them. Ella's not safe in that house with them—or her dad."

"Not safe with Edgar and Ceil?" Her voice soars up the tension scale.

"Ceil turned into a wolf and attacked Esmeralda, and probably the Pearlys' dog, and maybe she even sucked the blood out of a seagull." There, I said it. But I can tell the seagull part didn't help my argument.

Mom's face is getting redder by the second. She rubs her eyes with her fingertips and shakes her head.

"I honestly don't know what to say. It's not like we haven't been down this path before, with wild accusations." Her voice shifts to a monotone. "There are no vampires in Maiden Rock, Quinnette. Edgar and Ceil are not vampires. Nor are they attacking animals or sucking anyone's blood, including cats, dogs, or seagulls. And if I hear you saying that around town, you are grounded for the rest of the summer. That means, no hanging around with Ella and Ben . . . or Dominic. We'll find you something to do at the café that will keep you busy and out of trouble."

I contemplate no Ella, no Ben, and most of all, no Dominic—but I can't stop myself from arguing back. "Mom, what if they—"

"No, Quinnette. I don't want to hear another word about this. No harassing Edgar and Ceil. Leave them alone. Let them enjoy the peace and quiet they came here for. Are we clear?"

Only one answer to this will keep me in normal human society. "Yes."

The last thing Mom does before I leave the room is turn on her body cam, point to the lens and then to me, and say, "I'm watching you."

## 2I

Okay, that didn't go as well as I would have liked. But one thing I know is, you can't kill an idea once it's landed soundly in your head. And the idea that Edgar and Ceil are vampires is in Mom's head now too, and it will buzz around until it has a place to land. I know her. She'll come around, somehow, some way.

I check my phone for reports.

Ella: *Quiet here.*

Ben: *It would be quiet here except for the L.L.Bean geeks roaming the beach.*

Dominic: *I resent that. These guys give geeks a bad name.*

Ella: *What? Where are they?*

Ben: *Walking up and down the beach.*

Ella: *By my house?*

Dominic: *Just walked within twenty feet of us.*

Ben: *I think I heard one of them fart. Is that close enough?*

Ella: *I can't believe this.*

Something familiar creeps along the back of my neck. Suspicion. As if I don't have enough to worry about, the L.L.Bean boys are turning into celebrity stalkers. I want to run downstairs and tell Mom, but I know for sure it's not a good time.

Me: *Can you guys get a picture of them near Ella's house? So it's clear they're acting stalkery?*

Dominic: *Absolutely.*

Ella: *Where did they say they were from?*

Me: *Ohio, I think. They own electronic cigarette stores.*

Ella: *They don't look like they'd be Transylvanian Drip fans.*

Me: *What do you think TD fans look like?*

Ella: *I don't know. Not like that.*

Me: *Maybe they're vampire hunters.*

Dominic: *Ha! Could be. I'll google vampire hunting and see if they use fishing rods.*

Me: *Funny.*

Ella: *These guys are too stupid to be vampire hunters.*

Dominic: *You don't have to be Einstein to believe you can slay bloodthirsty hellions.*

* * *

I sit on the edge of my bed and think about vampire slayers. If I had to describe one before today, I would have said hip, leather-clad, good hair—no, great hair. Definitely not paunchy, old guy, sloppy eater who wears the same fishing-catalogue clothes every day. But what an amazing cover if John and Bob are for real? Who would guess that a couple of clueless auto-graph seekers are fighting for the side of the angels? But then again, maybe they're just annoying celebrity stalkers, and that's all.

Following Dominic's lead, I grab my tablet and google "vampire slayers." Within seconds, up pops hundreds of pictures of hip, handsome, leather-clad, good—no, *great*—haired young people. And what's more, half of them are girls. But not one of them looks like the L.L.Bean boys in any way. Still . . . the perfect cover would outwit a Google search.

A creak from the stairs gives me a much-needed distraction. I know it's Mom's footsteps by the sound of the heavy sheriff's shoe. A light tap on my door comes next.

"Quinnie?"

"What?"

"Can I come in?" As usual, she opens the door as she says this. "I've been thinking about our talk . . ."

I knew it.

"And I think it must be because Blythe has you reading those vampire books. It gets your imagination going—"

I sit bolt upright. "This is not Ms. Stillford's fault, if that's what you mean."

"I'm just trying to understand."

"You will. I just hope it's before I have four pointy teeth."

She rolls her eyes. "Good night, Quinnette. Remember what I said."

When she's gone and the door is firmly shut, I'm glad I at least bit my tongue about John and Bob being vampire hunters. Before I say anything to Mom, I need proof. Hard evidence that John and Bob are on the hunt for the real deal. Or I'll be grounded until my clothes go out of style.

*  *  *

The next morning, we're on the case early—minus poor Ben, who has another day of school. But crazy us, we start out by going back to Ms. Stillford's. We find her in her potting shed with flats of mulch and packets of seeds. We ask her what she knows about John and Bob.

"They seem like nice enough fellows. I think

Maiden Rock has made a good impression on them," Ms. Stillford says.

I pause, trying to think of a way to ask her what else she knows about them without her thinking that we're going to harass the two guys that all the grown-ups like so much—and without her mentioning it to Mom. But she knows me too well.

"Okay, what are you guys up to?"

"Nothing," I say.

Ms. Stillford laughs. "You kids need something to do. How about cleaning out my carriage house? I'll let you sell any old junk in there in a tag sale, and you can keep half the profits."

On any other day of my life, this would be a terrific offer. There is so much cool stuff in that carriage house. But we have important business to get on with.

"Thanks, Ms. Stillford. Can we do it in a couple weeks?"

"Sure, sure," she says. "Go blow off some steam for a while."

On the way back around Circle Lane, Ella's still wrestling with the situation and getting frustrated with our lack of answers. "If those guys really are vampire hunters, they don't look like a match for my aunt and uncle. And if they're not, they should get the heck away from here."

"We can't exactly walk up to them in Gusty's and ask them if they're friends of Buffy," Dominic says.

"I wonder what's really in those gear bags they carry around," I say, "or in their room at Miss Wickham's?"

Dominic looks at me. "Why do I think we're about to find out?"

Ella laughs. "Ah, you know her so well already."

"So what is my mission?" Dominic says. "Bag rifling?"

"Well," I say, "you can choose. You and Ben can follow the vampires or the goofballs. Which do you want?"

Dominic doesn't hesitate. "Vampires."

"Fine. Ella and I will poke around for intel on the goofballs."

* * *

During the next two days, Ella and I spend as much time as we can at Gusty's when John and Bob are there. We move around. Sit where we can hear their conversations. We walk around Circle Lane and stroll past Miss Wickham's when their car is out front. We walk under the open window we think is their room. We ask around. Not too obvious-like. People tell us what they think. After two days, we summarize our notes:

*Autograph Hounds or Vampire Hunters?*

*Subjects: John and Bob from Ohio*

*Known Facts: They drive a car with Ohio license plates. It's a dusty green Honda. They are staying at Miss Wickham's in room 211. They wear clothes from L.L.Bean—the same ones every day. They carry gear bags. They eat at Gusty's three times a day. They appear friendly and they joke with people in town. They walk on the beach morning and night. They've looked in some house windows. They've walked by Ella's house several times. They've driven down Mile Stretch Road at least two times a day. They've stopped near Ella's house. They fish (or pretend to fish) on the beach at odd hours with the wrong fishing gear. They've walked around the yacht club and looked at boats at least three times. They've been seen digging in Ella's trash bins.*

*Things that cannot be confirmed: They own electronic cigarette stores in Ohio. They really want to explore Maine. They're seriously interested in real estate in Maiden Rock. What's in their gear bags?*

*People they have asked about the famous vampire writers (that we know of): Margaret Boyd, Quinnie Boyd, John Denby, and Dominic Moldarto.*

Two copies come off the printer, and I hand one to Ella. We proofread.

During the time that Ella and I followed John and Bob, Ben and Dominic watched Edgar and Ceil. The only excitement they had was when John and Bob came up the beach in the dark and started digging in the trash bins at the back of Ella's house. Otherwise, Ceil took two early evening strolls on the beach, and no pets turned up drained.

I let the paper float to my bed. "Do you think they're looking for some*body*? Or some*thing*? I think they're looking for some*thing*."

"In our trash. In the dark. It's so"—Ella shivers—"creepy."

"But they haven't made a move to go inside. They're keeping their distance."

"All I can say is, if they're looking for fan stuff to sell on the Internet, like something with my aunt or uncle's writing on it, they're playing with fire."

"Sure, but if that's what they're doing, they don't know they're playing with fire because they don't know Edgar and Ceil are vampires."

"I'm becoming more convinced they're crazy stalker paparazzi," Ella says. "Maybe you should show this to your mom, and she'll investigate it for their own good."

"And tell her what? That Edgar and Ceil need protection from some fishermen?"

"Come on, Q. That they are paparazzi." Her green eyelids open wide. "She would believe that, right? Your mom would *have to* check that out."

"They don't have cameras."

"What if we said they were stalkers?"

"That might work. We've seen stranger things around here."

* * *

I have our investigative notes rolled up behind my back when I walk downstairs the next morning. I've changed the title to: *Suspicious Activities Report.* Mom is in the kitchen making toast.

"Morning, Mom."

"Good morning, Quinnie. Toast?"

"No thanks. I'm going to the café." I lean on the counter, squeezing the paper so hard it's starting to scrunch. "Mom, I wanted to talk to you about something. Again."

I hold out the Suspicious Activities Report, which is now twisted in the middle.

"What's this?"

"Just read it. Then I'll explain."

Her shoulders sag when she reads the title. I want to read over her shoulder but I stand back. Once she's reading it a second time, I move a couple inches closer. Finally, she sits down at the table and lays the report in front of her.

"You saw them all these times around the Philpotts'?"

"Me, and Ella, and Ben, and Dominic."

"Uh-*huh*. Who saw them picking in the Philpotts' trash bins?"

"Ben and Dominic."

"And who saw them fishing in that area?"

"All of us."

"How do you know they asked John Denby about Edgar and Ceil?"

"He told Ben that."

"And Dominic?"

"It was at Gusty's. I was there."

Mom clearly believes our report is worth something. Otherwise, she wouldn't even be asking questions. But there is still the possibility that she will blow up. At least she hasn't asked the exact times of any of these observations. Although we probably should have noted that in the report anyway. I mean, trash-digging late at night is more suspicious than trash-digging in the daytime.

"You do realize that you've done exactly what you promised you wouldn't do?"

"Yes, but."

"Yes, but, what?"

I search for the right words. "I haven't harassed Edgar and Ceil."

"Well, there's a consolation." Mom gets up and adjusts her sheriff's belt. "I'm disappointed, Quinn. Do you know why?"

"But, Mom. They're the ones harassing Edgar and Ceil. They're paparazzi or something. Paparazzi have killed people, chasing them for pictures."

She repeats her last question: "Do you know why I'm disappointed?"

I know what she wants to hear. "Fine. I should have told you first."

"Bingo. You should have come to me and let me do the investigation." She tosses her toast in the trash and wipes the counter. "Don't follow them around anymore. Do you understand?"

"Are you going to do something?" I ask.

"Are you going to answer my question?"

"Fine. I won't follow them around anymore."

"I'll look into this." She walks toward her office, and I follow her. "By the way, when were they picking through the Philpotts' trash?"

Gulp. I have to say it. At least this way, Mom's sure to jump on the case. "It might have been about two a.m."

She touches her hair like thinking this through hurts her brain. "So you were running a stakeout by Ella's house all night long?"

"Not me, exactly." I hate to put this on Ben and Dominic, but . . .

"Then who?"

## 22

That afternoon, all four of us are lined up in the Boyd family living room, being lectured about "unauthorized investigations, harassing John and Bob, violating curfew, and frolicking on the beach at night while a dangerous coyote is at large in the vicinity." I thought Mom might have cooled off a bit during the day, but she seems to have gotten more wound up while waiting for the other grown-ups to arrive.

John Denby paces around the room. Ben is *grounded*. The Moldartos have folded their arms across their chests so tightly, they look like their circulation is suffering. Dominic will be *confined to quarters*. And, of course, Mr. Philpotts is there too, completely deadpan. He listens to Mom and shakes his head back and forth.

When it's over, Ben and his uncle leave, but not before John Denby cuffs Ben on the back of the head. Dominic's parents march him out between the two of them, single file. But before Mr. Philpotts leaves with Ella, Mom says, "Wait. I'd like to talk to you."

Mr. Philpotts sits down in a comfy chair, waiting for Mom to speak. It's hard to tell whether he's upset about this or if his mind is back in his office on a detective story he was interrupted from writing.

"Jack, I wish the children hadn't been up to these antics, but the fact is, I have to check into this. It looks like these characters are casing your house."

"I don't like it either, Margaret. Do you have any idea whether it's because of Edgar and Ceil, or could it be me they're stalking? *I've* got some unstable fans too, I'm sure."

Mom looks a little embarrassed that she might have insulted him. "Yes, of course. Sure, it could be fans of yours too. I was only thinking since they were asking about Edgar and Ceil—"

"You're probably right." He looks like he's going to get up to leave.

"One more thing," Mom says. "I'd like to come by tomorrow morning and meet with Edgar and Ceil as part of my investigation."

"Sure. I'll tell them."

Mom relaxes a little and gives Mr. Philpotts the sign he can leave. Before he does, Ella says, "Dad, I'd feel better staying here with Quinnie tonight."

He looks at Mom. She nods her head as if the idea makes a lot of sense. "Go upstairs. Now, girls."

*Good move, Ella,* I'm thinking.

Ella and I hang out at the bottom of the stairs long enough to hear Mom tell Mr. Philpotts he should make sure all the doors and windows are locked and the curtains drawn in the evening. From the tone of her voice, I can tell she's concerned.

Once Ella and I head up to my room, I flop onto the bed while she paces and checks her phone.

"It's only five thirty." She raises a fingernail to her teeth as if she's about to take a nervous bite, but then she checks the polish and stops herself.

"And?"

"And I'm wondering if the L.L.Bean boys are away from their room at Miss Wickham's. They're probably at Gusty's, eating."

"You want to sneak into their room now?"

"Of course I do. Don't you?"

I sit up. "I guess I do. We might find what they took out of your trash. And that might tell us more about why they're here, because if they're *not* paparazzi . . . they might be vampire hunters, and then . . ."

". . . they're here to do a really sad kind of good. And maybe they need help."

Ella's being so brave, I want to hug her. But she's also being a little unrealistic.

"It's a good idea, but we'd have to sneak in without Miss Wickham seeing us and then somehow get into their room—assuming we're right about which room is theirs."

I can tell the wheels are spinning in Ella's head. She raises my window and presses her cheek against the screen, assessing the distance to the ground below.

"Oh, yeah," I add. "And we also need to get out of *this* house without getting caught."

Ella carefully opens my door and listens. Her dad's still here, but he and my mom have reached our front hallway.

"Let me know, Jack," Mom says. "I'd like to stop by at about nine tomorrow morning."

"Okay, Margaret. I'll confirm with you."

Ella and I venture into sight so she can say goodbye. Her dad peers up over his glasses at us and says, "Do you need anything for tonight?"

Ella says, "No, I can borrow whatever from Quinnie."

"Well, stay in the house, El, and call me before you go to sleep." Mr. Philpotts is normally a pretty serious-looking man, but now his face is even stiffer.

"Okay, Dad," Ella says. "You be safe too."

The front door hasn't quite closed behind Mr. Philpotts when Mom turns to us. "Come on down, girls."

Ella and I don't groan out loud, but it feels like we're marching to our sentencing. But—surprise, surprise—when we reach Mom's office, she wants more details. She even wants us to show her where John and Bob fished, where they drove, and what houses they looked in, and she wants the video of them picking in the trash. She takes notes and presses the button on her body camera.

It worked. She might not believe that Ceil and Edgar are vampires, but I can tell she'll be monitoring these two suspicious guys. That could be enough to crack this wide open and keep everybody safe. But before we're completely finished downloading our evidence for her, she gets a call that clearly annoys her.

She stuffs the phone in her pocket without even swiping it off. "I have to go to Rook River. There's a ten car pileup south of town on Highway 72A."

Ella and I look at each other and try to control the *yay!* we are feeling. Our investigation just got easier. Then I think, yikes, accident. "Anybody hurt?" I ask.

"Doesn't look too bad, but they need people to assess the scene and take reports. You guys go to the café for dinner and then come right back here. No frolic and detour. Got it?"

"Got it," I say.

Ella looks at me like, *What the heck is a frolic and detour?* I half-wave like I'll explain it later.

We start hustling to the café, but before we set foot in the parking lot, John and Bob come out and head for their green Honda. We pause on the side of the road and watch them. Bob opens the driver's-side door, burps into his fist, and adjusts his cap before he climbs in. John runs his thumbs around his belt like he's trying to make more room, then throws his body into the passenger seat and struggles with the seat belt. I have to admit: this . . . does not seem quite like vampire-slayer behavior.

The Honda engine turns over, and Bob yanks the wheel to the right. Ella and I watch as the car passes us and cruises down Mile Stretch Road, rolls through the stop sign in front of my house, and turns to head out of town.

"Are you thinking what I'm thinking?" Ella says.

"If we're gonna do it, we better get going."

I check the Gusty's parking lot. It's almost full. And Clooney Wickham's car is in its usual spot. This means only Miss Wickham would be at the bed-and-breakfast. And who knows, maybe *she's* not even there. With so many people to serve, Dad won't notice if I'm thirty minutes late.

I start to run. Ella is on my heels. We're almost at Circle Lane when we hear a car approaching from behind us. We dive into the nearest bushes.

"Oh, no," Ella moans. "They're back."

I crouch down and look at the car coming. "Can't be, unless they forgot something or changed their minds."

The car slows at the entrance to the lane and turns slowly toward the yacht club. Whew—it's Ms. Stillford's old Volvo.

Ella pulls at my arm. "Let's go."

We thrash through the wooded area and come out the other side, facing the B&B.

Lights are on in the lobby, the front door is open, and through the screen door, we can see Miss Wickham sorting papers at the front desk. Ella darts to the outer edge of the porch, and I follow. She points to two windows on the second floor.

"I think that's their room."

"We can't climb two stories," I say. There's nothing but a narrow ledge about ten feet up.

"But the second window is open!"

"Hello? What would we climb on?"

Ella ignores my last question, scanning the side yard for something like a ladder. I decide to crawl across the front porch and sneak a peek at the front desk. My head is about a foot off the floor when I look inside.

Miss Wickham is talking to herself while she scribbles on a pad and turns pages over and over. She looks up. I duck. She goes back to scribbling. I lean in again. She grabs the all papers and straightens them with a tap on the bottom, a tap on the side, then on the bottom again. Then she walks around the desk and down the hall to the dining room. I want to scream, "*Ella!*" but instead I jump up, run to the side, and wave my arms like windmills trying to get her attention.

A second later, we are inside the B&B, straight through the front door and bolting for the stairway. It *eeks* and *squeaks*, but we streak up to the second floor, barely touching the steps.

## 23

The glass lamps in the upstairs hallway cast an eerie light. The wooden floor is so warped, we go up and down like we're walking on a wave. The blistered rose wallpaper smells of mildew.

Ella grabs for the first doorknob on the right—the one she is convinced Miss Wickham rented to the L.L.Bean guys. A *Do Not Disturb* sign hangs around the handle. Her hand twists the knob, without success. I run down the hall, trying the other knobs. Locked. Locked. Locked. The next one I grab turns to the right. I pull on the door, and it opens to reveal a cleaning closet, complete with an old-timey maid's cart and feather duster.

My eyes catch the glint of metal.

"Ella," I whisper hoarsely. "Look." I hold up a ring filled with classic-looking curlicued keys.

The keys jingle as I run to Ella.

"Hurry," she whispers. It takes us three tries to find the right one.

*Snap. Click.* The keyhole says yes to us.

Ella turns the doorknob and pushes against the old paneled wood. At first it sticks, then suddenly it gives way, revealing a large guest room. I run on my tiptoes to return the keys to the cart.

We slip in the guys' guest room, leaving the door ajar so we can hear if anyone comes up the stairs.

The bed, the dresser, the braid rug are all vintage—I mean the rug is *seriously* vintage, as in a gazillion years old and threadbare. Flowered curtains sag over the windows and pitchers bursting with artificial flowers sit on the nightstands.

I tiptoe my way around the room. Shirts are crumpled on the top of the dresser, shoes scattered around the floor. A film of whisker hair mars the bathroom sink.

"One suspicion confirmed," Ella says as she holds up two large, empty L.L.Bean shopping bags.

Next, she opens the closet door and points inside. A leather jacket's dangling, one shoulder on the hanger and one off. It almost looks like it's trying to make a getaway.

"Another non-surprise: slobs," I tell Ella. I've spotted a stack of Gusty's take-out boxes on the radiator. The top one is flipped open, and a crab cake sandwich inside is growing green hair. In a wastebasket next to the radiator lies a plastic shopping bag. For some reason, the handles are tied into a knot. I lift it, untie the top, and look in. The bag's filled with wadded tissues, used dental floss, a hairbrush with a broken handle, and an empty bottle of Cobalt Cabana Blue nail polish. I can barely get the word out. "Look!"

Ella rushes over and picks out the polish bottle— with fingertips of the same color. Her voice cracks. "What do they want with this?"

"Maybe they sell celebrity garbage. Like on eBay."

"This isn't Aunt Ceil's trash," Ella says. "It's mine!"

"They may have figured that out, and that's why it's in the wastebasket."

Ella picks the bag up and walks across the room.

"What are you doing?" I ask.

"It's my trash, and I'm taking it back."

I'm just about ready to conclude—for good— that these slobs are unscrupulous dealers in celebrity mementos, when Ella says, "Check this out." She's leaning over a small oak table. "They've definitely been tracking somebody. It has to be Edgar and Ceil."

Spread out on the tablecloth is a map of New England, with red circles around certain towns. The circled towns form a bunch of lines, like the spokes on a bike wheel, jutting out from New York City in several northerly directions. One trail of towns leads to Lake Winnipesaukee, New Hampshire; one to Otisville, New York; one to Montpelier, Vermont; and one to Rook River, Maine.

"Maybe they've been following four different people," I say.

"Maybe they went in each of those directions before they came here," Ella says.

"Don't touch the map," I whisper. "It's evidence."

I hear hinges creak downstairs, and I freeze— that'd be the screen door to the B&B. Voices drift upstairs. It's the Morgans and their grandkids. Mrs. Morgan is asking about six rooms for a family reunion. I look at Ella. She's not moving either. I try to take a gentle step, but the floorboard underneath my flip-flop groans like it has a toothache. We're stuck like statues until they leave.

Leave. Leave. Please, please leave.

The sound of a car pulling up comes next. I can't even see outside to know whether the car is here at the B&B or over at the pound, or if the car is Mom's. Her mom antennae can practically find me anywhere.

Worse, what if the car is John and Bob's? They may have forgotten something and turned around.

The door to the B&B opens again.

"Hi, George. When'd you get here?"

"Merle, buddy! Good to see you."

It's more summer people. They fall into a conversation with Mr. Morgan, while their grandkids squeal and run around. I consider whether the talking downstairs will mask any noise we might make walking upstairs.

The grandkids' voices get closer. Oh, no. One of them is on the stairway.

"Pop Pop, what's up here?"

The window to the B&B's side yard is open. I consider running across the room and diving out of it, but that would put me in the garden with a broken neck.

"Here, here," says Mr. Morgan. "Come down. That's not your business. Carol, we need to get these kids to the beach."

"The beach, the beach," they yell over each other.

Someone, probably Mr. Morgan, opens the screen door, and the voices fade.

The knot in my throat slowly relaxes, and after a few much-needed breaths, I wave to Ella that we should go. But she turns and starts digging wildly through the duffel bags. When she pushes back the clothes inside them, there, in the bottom of one bag, face up, is the familiar cover of *Transylvanian Drip*. Ella lifts it out and opens the cover. Inside is a hand-scratched note that says: *Buddy Denton Show—Victoria Kensington is Edgar Waterman and Ceil Waterman.* We look at each other and nod like, *Okay, now we're on to something!*

Ella stuffs the book back in the bag, but not before she sees a scrap of paper tucked deep into the pages. She pulls it out. "OMG! This is Aunt Ceil's handwriting."

She sticks the paper in my face, so close that I can't read it. I push her hand away and scan the scrawl of purple ink across the scrap paper. It looks like a signature, or at least part of a signature, that ends in *—aterman.*

"Why do they have her signature?" Ella says. "Did she write to them? Does she know them?"

I try not to yell. "Put the book back! Just like it was!"

Now Ella's fingerprints are on the book and the note! Mom is going to kill me. But at this second, that's the least of my worries.

We have only one way out. Old buddy Merle is still downstairs. Now he's talking to Miss Wickham about the weather—which can take an hour, around these parts. So we don't have a choice. We'll have to climb out the window, onto the narrow ledge, drop down to the ground, and run for it.

By the time my brain processes this, Ella is half out the window already. The bright blue of her nail polish atop the window frame is the last thing I see before she hisses, "*Come on.*"

The B&B door creaks below, and John and Bob's voices ring through the lobby as they say hello to Miss Wickham. I'm up and out the window in a split second.

"Back so soon?" Miss Wickham says.

"Forgot my wallet," John says.

I look down. Whoa. It's only the second story, I tell myself.

Ella bark-whispers, "Help."

She's hovering to my right, balanced on the ledge with her belly flat against the building. Her right hand's grasping the thin grooves between the clap-board siding, and her other hand's holding the plastic trash bag. I inch next to her. My senses sharpen. I can hear my clothes brushing against the wall. Feel the salty air on my face. Hear the squirrel scurrying up the tree ten feet in front of us.

Ella might have been the first one outside, but

she's turned pale as an eggshell. We stare in each other's eyes, neither of us wanting to look down again.

And then John and Bob's voices float out of the window next to us. I may be standing on a ledge, about to do a backward swan dive, but I'm not going to pass up a chance to gather more intel. So I mouth to Ella, *Hold still.*

# 24

"What the . . . ?"

"What?"

"Somebody's been in here."

"Who?"

"Probably the witch who owns this place."

"Did she take anything?"

"I'm looking."

"We should make a report to the lady sheriff."

They both break into laughter, then one of them says, "Naw. We need to get what we came for and get outta this miserable, godforsaken lobstertown."

For a second, I think I'm losing my footing, and I grab for Ella's arm but it's flailing in the air, and soon the ancient ledge is crumbling beneath our weight. We crash into the chokecherry bushes, scramble to our feet, and run frantically around Circle Lane toward Gusty's.

"Did you hear what they said?" I'm breathing hard as I run. "'We need to get what we came for and get outta this miserable, godforsaken lobstertown.'"

"What they came for?" Ella says. "What does that mean?"

"I don't know!" I veer toward the Gusty's parking lot, but Ella pulls me forward with a look of determination on her face.

"Well, obviously they know Aunt Ceil." She holds up the scrap of paper with Ceil's signature on it.

"You took that?" I yelp. "That's evidence!"

"Yes, I took it, and I'm going to show it to Aunt Ceil right now and demand to know exactly what's going on here. Who these guys are, what she did to Esmeralda, all of it."

"I don't know," I tell her. "What if she gets angry, and . . ."—I can't stop myself—". . . the fangs come out?"

"That's not going to happen. I'm safe with her," Ella says. "I still believe that. She'll talk to me."

*  *  *

I don't have time to think about the fact that Mom set up a meeting with Edgar and Ceil for tomorrow morning, and that I'm about to interfere with her investigation *again*. I just go-go-go. Along the way, Ella and I see Dominic sitting on his front porch.

We slow down only slightly as we pass him.

"Yo!" Dominic calls. "Anybody answer their texts anymore?"

I grab my phone from my pocket.

There are four texts from Dominic. They add up to: *I got news!*

He starts to rise, but Ella holds up her hand in traffic-cop position. "Not now, okay? Quinnie and I are on a mission. I promise we'll text you when we're done."

He points to the trash bag in her hand. "What's that?"

"*This* is my trash, which I have reclaimed. Now, we've got to go."

His face drops, and he goes back to staring at passing cars. "Okay, but you're going to be sorry."

I come to a full stop. "Why?"

"Well," he says with a cagey grin. "The minute we left your house, my parents made me go with them to the B&B to ask about rooms for my aunt and uncle and three cousins for the Fourth of July, and while Miss Wickham took them in the dining room to tell them all about her menu"—Dominic waves a piece of paper—"I managed to get these."

I run over to him and grab the papers. They're photocopies of John and Bob's registration form and driver's licenses. The B&B registration form is all in scribble writing. The first name looks like John Smith. The other one looks like Bob Jones. The address on the form looks like: *43 Sprofgjuld, Colbomush OH*. No zip.

I want to hug him! "Oh, man, Dominic. This is great!"

Ella looks over my shoulder. "You'd only write like this if you were trying to hide your identity," she says.

"Look at the other page," Dominic says.

Ella and I put our heads together to study the second piece of paper, the one with photocopies of Indiana driver's licenses. John Smith's address is 123 Rosebud Lane, Greenfield IN, 46117. Bob Jones's address is 124 Rosebud Lane, Greenfield IN, 46117.

"Fake IDs," Ella and I say at the same time.

"Fake IDs," Dominic agrees. He looks at me like, *So, what's up?*

"Well, we went to the B&B too," Ella hurries to say. "It must have been right after you were there." She starts to walk, and I fall in step.

"What did you find out?" Dominic follows us.

"We got in their room and found a map of New England. It had a bunch of towns between here and New York circled in red," I say.

We're walking three abreast now.

"And other routes to other towns too," Ella says. "One in upstate New York, one in New Hampshire, and one in Vermont."

I butt in. "But the biggest thing we found was a copy of *Transylvanian Drip* in one of their duffel bags, and it had a scribbled note inside that said something about how Victoria Kensington is Edgar and Ceil."

"And there was a scrap of paper with part of Aunt Ceil's signature on it." Ella closes her eyes like she's picturing it.

"Wowza," says Dominic.

"And then the Morgans brought their grand-kids into the B&B, then some other summer people came in—"

Ella interrupts me: "*And then* the L.L.Bean boys came back."

"And we were trapped," I say.

"And we had no choice," she says. "We had to go out the window."

Dominic holds up his hands. "So what's the verdict? Are they paparazzi, stalkers, or vampire hunters?"

"They're . . . something," I tell him.

"Yep. Something more than autograph seekers," Ella adds. "Now we're going to see my aunt and uncle and find out what's really going on," Ella says.

Dominic waves the photocopies and says, "I do believe I've earned my right to go along."

"What about your parents? Aren't you confined to your house?" I ask.

"They're at work," Dominic says and laughs. "Plus, didn't you blow your house arrest already?"

# 25

When we hurry into Ella's house, she finds her dad writing at his desk. "Hey," I hear her say. "Writing," he replies.

After Ella finds a wastebasket and dumps her reclaimed trash, the three of us walk through to the kitchen. Outside the window, the dune's mass of feathery sea grass is blowing in the wind. Gray clouds are forming over the ocean. Ella opens the cabinet and pulls out a package of Oreos, and I immediately gobble down three. Dominic swallows a dose of four. After all, we're on the verge of confronting Edgar and Ceil about just exactly who they are. And this requires fortifying ourselves with chocolate cookies.

The kitchen door creaks, and Ceil peers in on us. "I thought I heard you kids." She's thin and weary-looking but stunning in black pants, a black sweater, red lips, and dark glasses. "I need coffee." She reaches for the Gusty's carafe, pops off the lid, and raises it to her nose. She inhales deeply, then pours a cup and drains the contents. "My life's blood."

Edgar glides in after her and takes a seat at the kitchen table. "A cup, Ceil, my love."

"Wait." Ella pauses, and I wonder how she's going to start. "Aunt Ceil? Uncle Edgar? Can we talk for a second?"

"Yes, lovie?" Ceil says.

"There is something you need to know—*I* need to know—I need to *ask*."

Ceil hears the shakiness in Ella's voice and puts her arm around Ella's shoulders. "What's the matter, El?"

Dominic and I shuffle uncomfortably. Seconds pass. Or a minute. Then Ella comes through with a big blurt.

"Are you guys vampires?"

It feels like the kitchen clock stops ticking, the refrigerator ceases humming, the icemaker halts mid-cube-making. An eternity passes in silence and then . . . Ceil laughs.

"It's not a joke!" Ella says. "You say you talk to vampires, you stay out of the light, you . . . you . . . cover the mirrors. You don't eat." Ella's on a roll. "Cats and gulls are being drained of blood since you came."

"Ella!" Edgar's deep voice stops her with a warning tone. His neck turns red with irritation. "We're *not* vampires."

"*Edgar,*" Ceil warns him.

"No, Ceil. This is too much," he argues back. "This is ridiculous."

But Ella's gathered her courage. "Prove it."

"How exactly would you like us to do that?" Ceil says.

"I don't care," Ella demands. "The usual way."

It crosses my mind that vampires have tricks for just such occasions.

"Fine," says Ceil hoarsely. "Get a cross, cook up some garlic, open the drapes, let in the sun, bring out a Bible." She pushes herself up from the table with her thin white fingers and slowly pulls her dark glasses away from her face.

It's cool white, and her eyes are . . . normal human eyes. Eyes that don't flinch in the light of the kitchen.

But Ella's not taking any chances. "Wait right here," she says, then backs to the door and bolts down the hall.

"Dad, do we have a Bible?" Ella yells.

The four of us stay frozen in place until Ella rushes back in, holding a black book with a gold cross on the cover. She thrusts it at Ceil like she's offering a gift. A chance for Ceil to prove herself.

Ceil sighs and takes it.

In a slightly ceremonial way, she raises her hand and places it over the cross. Edgar reaches over and places his hand over hers. In unison, they look at Ella.

Dominic, Ella, and I look at their hands.

No smoke rises, no flesh sears, no flames erupt. No screaming, writhing, or melting takes place.

"So?" says Ceil. "Did we pass?"

Ella dissolves into tears and rushes to Ceil, who wraps her in her arms. Dominic and I both let out deep breaths.

"Honey, we couldn't tell you. It's our arrangement with our publisher. We agreed to say we talk to the Count—to keep some of the myth alive. Do you understand? It's marketing."

Mom's words echo in my head. *It's marketing.*

"But there are people following you," Ella gets out between sobs. "Why are they doing that?"

Ceil sits up. "What do you mean?"

Our intel tumbles out of Ella. "There are two men in town and they call themselves John Smith and Bob Jones and they say they are from Ohio and they own electronic cigarette stores and they're just here to fish, but they don't know how to fish, and they have fake IDs, and they dig in our trash, and they have a map that brought them here, and they have a copy of *Transylvanian Drip* in the bottom of their duffel bag and there's a note in it that says: *Buddy Denton Show—Victoria Kensington is Edgar Waterman and Ceil Waterman.*" She sucks in a huge breath. "And they have this." She thrusts the scrap of paper with Ceil's signature at her.

It's not exactly the way I would have explained the matter, but it definitely strikes a chord with Edgar and Ceil. Edgar rushes toward the garage while Ceil gets on her feet and heads upstairs.

"*Stop!*" Ella yells. "*Please.* Tell us what's going on."

Edgar and Ceil slowly turn around.

"What do these men look like?" Edgar asks.

Ben hands him the photocopy of the drivers' licenses.

"Oh, Ceil." Edgar hands her the paper. "It's them. The Woodleys."

"We really have to go," Ceil says to Ella.

"No," Ella says with a voice that means *NO*. "No one is going anywhere until we get the whole story, and I mean the *whole* story. Who are the Woodleys?"

"Maybe my mom can help" comes out of my mouth, while my head is thinking, *Now is the time to call the cops.*

"Oh, no." Edgar and Ceil shake their heads vigorously. "That's just a waste of time. We've been through too many police reports. They never do anything. No police, no sheriff. No law. They're useless."

"What? They won't do anything about what?" I ask.

Edgar sinks into a chair. "Show them, Ceil."

Ceil walks upstairs, gliding like a ghost, and returns with a handful of scrawled handwritten messages. She lays them on the table, and we each reach for one, read it, then pass it around. They all say pretty much the same thing.

John and Bob, aka Jack and Wally Woodley, claim to be friends and confidants of Count Le Plasma too. And they say he told them his stories first, and they say the Count demands that Edgar and Ceil give them "the dough from the cat in the van story."

"These guys are nutballs," says Dominic, "and crooks! Nutball crooks."

"Of course they are!" Ceil's agitated again. "But they keep writing us and emailing us and sending messages to our fan-mail PO box."

"And you called the police?" I ask—carefully, so it doesn't sound like I didn't hear them the first time. I just want to be clear about *what* they told the police.

"It's all so awful," Ceil whispers and puts her face in her hands.

There were never three kids more interested in the complete explanation of "awful" than the three of us. Ella, Dominic, and I sit perfectly still, waiting for the details. Edgar and Ceil both start talking at once, and it begins to pour out.

"We have lots of fans who think they're vampires, or want to be vampires, or want to be around vampires."

"When the Woodley brothers told us they also talked to the Count, we thought, *whatever*, and figured it would pass."

"Then they started demanding money."

"Which is when I wrote them a letter. That's how they came to have the scrap with my signature that you found. Like I said, our contract with our publisher says we can't reveal that we don't actually talk to the Count. It's the myth that sold the books. We have to take the public position—at all times—that we are his friends and storytellers."

"So Ceil wrote the Woodleys and explained we had received no such instruction from the Count and that we would not pay them anything."

"Which is when we started to get ugly threats."

"Gruesome threats."

"So we went to the NYPD and told them what we could."

I don't want to interrupt, but I have to ask, "What do you mean, 'what we could'?"

"Well, we didn't want to violate our contract. So we said, 'We write these books. Here they are. We have two crazed fans,' and we showed the police the letters and emails."

"What did they say?" Ella asks.

"They rolled their eyes and said we should make an official complaint for stalking and terroristic threats, and they'd open a case and investigate it."

"What'd they find out?" Dominic asks.

"Nothing. They couldn't identify the senders. They couldn't find anything."

"But you sent them a letter. Did they check that address?" I ask.

"Yes. But it was a PO Box in Brooklyn, opened under a false name."

I tell them, "You *have* to tell my mom."

"Sorry," Edgar says. "We've had enough of being laughed at by law enforcement. We're just going to leave. These people can't hound us forever. They'll lose interest. They'll take up after some unsuspecting zombie writers."

Ceil hesitates but then nods. "He's right. She'll

only think we're crackpots like the others did."

I'm about to say, *she will not!* when Edgar points his bony finger at me. "Quinnette, you are not to say a word to your mother about this. Do you understand? Will you respect our wishes? This matter is ours to deal with."

"Err, we've all told our parents we think these guys are spying on you," Dominic says.

"Oh, no." Ceil rubs her eyes and shakes her head. "Please. Not another word to anyone. Ella, please don't tell your father either. We'll inform him when we're ready."

I want to respect their wishes and leave it to them, but I think they need to know something. "My mom is coming here tomorrow to talk to you about John and Bob. She wants to warn you. She wants to investigate."

## 26

The next thing I know, Edgar and Ceil are tossing their things in suitcases. Ella brings a tube of toothpaste, then a bottle of shampoo, but she's mostly in the way. Ceil gives her a hug and tells her to sit.

"Where are you going?" I ask.

"Don't know, but it's time to leave Maiden Rock," says Edgar.

"I don't think you can just drive out of town in the Flying Spur and not get noticed," Dominic says.

That stops them both.

"John and Bob are all over this town," I add. "You can't just drive out, especially in that car, without being seen."

"How about leaving town in a boat?" Ella says. "Ben could help us. He can get one."

Everything in me says *tell Mom, tell Mom, tell Mom*. But I don't want to lose Ceil and Edgar's trust, and I don't want Ella to think I've betrayed them. I search my brain for options. The boat idea isn't a bad one. I mean, after all, they have a right to leave town any way they want. They're not the stalkers; they're the stalk-*ees*.

Ceil laughs. "We couldn't drive a toy boat around a bathtub."

"Thanks, but I don't think so, El," Edgar says.

Ella looks a little hurt.

Dominic says, "What if Ben drives the boat?"

"Maybe, but where could he take them?" Ella asks.

And that is seriously worth asking. Edgar, Ceil, and Ben would be leaving the tidal pool in a small boat headed into the open ocean in the middle of the night with no plan.

Edgar and Ceil shake their heads. "We won't involve you children in this. It's our problem."

My brain performs the perfect backflip and comes up with the solution. "I know where they'd go, and I know who'd take them there."

All eyes are on me, but I'm not worried. This is a kid-free boat plan: "It's really simple. We'll have the sisters pick up Edgar and Ceil here, using the convent van, and drive them up to the yacht club. Sister Rosie will turn around and drive back to Pidgin Beach, and Sister Ethel will take them in a boat down the coast to the lighthouse. There you can meet back up with Sister Rosie and be on your way!"

"And I could drive the Flying Spur down to Pidgin Beach, and it would be there for them," Dominic says, a little too hopefully.

"No one will be driving the Flying Spur but me," Edgar says.

"Then just leave it here, like a decoy," says Dominic.

"That's good. The car will stay in the garage," Ella says, "but between the nuns' van and the boat, we can still get them to the lighthouse, and we'll figure out how to get them on their way from there tomorrow."

"We can't do this tonight," I say. "The sisters don't even know about it."

"Then tomorrow night. We'll do it tomorrow night," Ella says. "That will give us twenty-four hours to convince the sisters and get everything in place."

Everyone looks at Edgar and Ceil for their agreement.

"Wait one minute," Edgar says. "Hiding in vans and riding in boats with nuns on the open ocean in the middle of the night?" He picks up his monogrammed Ballistic duffel bag and hoists it over his shoulder again. "I think not."

"He's right, children," says Ceil. "We have to do this our way."

"*Or . . .* ," Ella says, "we could tell my dad all of this. I'm sure he'd help."

Ceil looks alarmed. "We do not want to bring your father into this, Ella. Confiding in you kids has been stressful enough."

I follow Ella's lead. "Or my dad? We could tell my dad. I'm sure he would help, and he's not a police officer."

"Yeah," Dominic adds, "or we could get my parents. They're ocean scientists. They know a lot about the sea at night."

This flood of options seems to break down Edgar and Ceil's resistance. Edgar lets the bag slide off his shoulder. He leans against the doorframe with a deflated look on his face. "Suppose we consider your plan—and not because we can't do this ourselves—but suppose the sisters will help. When could we realistically get out of here?"

"I'm sure we can do it tomorrow night." I probably sound more confident than I am.

"That's just not good enough," Ceil says, biting at her red thumbnail.

"Aunt Ceil, it's only twenty-four hours," Ella says. "Just stay in the house for twenty-four more hours."

"Staying in the house isn't the problem," says Ceil. "Quinnie's mother is coming here to talk to us tomorrow morning. Isn't that what you said, Quinnie?"

The kitchen door squeaks open, and we all nearly jump out of our skin.

Mr. Philpotts sticks his head in. "What's going on in here?" He walks toward the latest supply of caffeine from Gusty's and finds it empty. He has a *lot* of catching up to do. "Ed, Ceil, what's with the luggage?" He appears to have just woken up from a deep afternoon sleep. I know this look. He's had his head deep in his computer, inventing the gory details of a crime.

All five of us fidget until Ella says, "Aunt Ceil and Uncle Edgar are going to go up to Bar Harbor for a few days."

Her dad scratches his head and yawns. "Is there any more coffee?"

"Sorry," says Ceil. "I got the last drop."

"Bar Harbor sounds like a good idea," says Mr. Philpotts. "Get out of Maiden Rock for a couple days. By the way, unless you're leaving tonight, Ed, Margaret Boyd, the sheriff, wants to stop by and talk to you tomorrow morning," says Ella's dad.

"So we've heard," says Ceil.

## 27

It would be best if Edgar and Ceil could leave tonight, but we have to talk to the sisters, talk to Ben, and think through the logistics. So we leave Edgar and Ceil to concentrate on what they will tell Mom in the morning. Dominic says he'll fill in Ben.

That night, after I say good night to Mom and Dad, I start shooting out to-do texts:

Me: *Tomorrow morning, Ben and Dominic go to the boathouse to get Ben's uncle's skiff ready.*

Ben: *On it.*

Dominic: *One hundred percent.*

Me: *Ella and I will get the sisters to help us.*

Ella: *Yep!*

Me: *A nautical map?*

Ben: *On it.*

Me: *Marine torch?*

Ben: *On it.*

I toss and turn all night. The ocean seems louder than usual, like it's trying to tell me to be careful. But I am being careful, I tell myself. Aren't I? I mean, none of us kids are going to be in the van with the sisters and Edgar and Ceil. Check. None of us will be in the boat with Sister Ethel, Edgar, and Ceil. Check. We haven't gone anywhere near John and Bob in person. Check. That is, if you don't count us being on the ledge outside their window when they came into their room. Nobody's doing anything illegal except the L.L.Bean boys, aka John and Bob, aka the Woodley brothers—crazed fans who got crazy enough to demand money from their favorite authors.

Still, I decide to get up and write Mom a note. I'll leave it for her so she won't find it until it's too late to stop the getaway.

*Mom,*

*I just wanted you to know that we talked to Edgar and Ceil, just like you did, and I'm not sure what they told you, but they know John and Bob. Actually, they know them as Jack and Wally Woodley. These guys are crazy fans who say they talked to Count Le Plasma, and that he wants Edgar and Ceil to give them all the money from the "cat in the van story," which would be Transylvanian Drip. Edgar and Ceil have tried to get help from the NYPD, but the police said it was kind of Edgar and Ceil's own fault for telling people they talk to vampires. We haven't mucked around in any police matter. We're helping Edgar and Ceil get out of town because they don't want police help and I guess that's their choice. I'm telling you everything I know.*

*Don't worry.*
*It's all cool.*
*Love,*
*Q*

There. That's good. I set it aside and plan to reread it in the morning. Always set a letter or email aside and let it rest before you send it. Ms. Stillford taught me that.

I feel more relaxed and put my cheek on my cool pillowcase. The next thing I know, it's morning.

* * *

Mom is adjusting her camera and her shoulder holster when I walk in the kitchen at eight o'clock.

"Wow. I thought you'd be sleeping in," she says.

"Nope. Too much to do."

"What's on your busy schedule?"

"Oh, we're going to hang out."

"You and Ella?"

"And Dominic and Ben." I look to see if she is scowling, but no.

"Ben's out of school now, too?"

"Uh-huh. Yesterday was his last day."

"I guess that's okay." She pauses like she's thinking it through. "But not in the evening. After dinner, back in the house. Okay?"

It pains me to do it, but in the interest of Ceil and Edgar's welfare, I lie. "Okay."

"Well, while you four are busy hanging out, could you assemble some of my welcome packets?"

I say, "Sure, Mom. Where's the stuff?" But I'm thinking, *I don't have time for this.* "Where are you going?"

"I have to go see Edgar and Ceil, then I have a training session in Rook River. I'll be back around five." She dusts her hands like she's satisfied she's fully and correctly assembled. "Everything you need is on the dining room table."

It's a good thing that she's wearing her uniform with the gun and camera and whole deal when she goes to see Edgar and Ceil. That should let them know she's more serious than the guys who laughed at them in Brooklyn.

Then, just as I think Mom's on her way, she stops. "Where are you headed right now?"

"Right this minute?"

"Yes, Quinnie, right this minute."

I wonder if she can detect my exponential fibbing. "Ella and I are going to the café for breakfast."

"Oh, good then." She gives me a quick hug and ruffles my hair, which I immediately smooth. "Those jeans are looking a little baggy. You should have two cinnamon buns." Her eyes pan down to my feet. "I thought you'd switched over to flip-flops for the summer."

I look at my feet. I'm wearing my oldest Top-Siders. They seemed serious enough for a serious day of maneuvers. "Oh, I don't know. I just didn't feel flip-floppy today."

She laughs. "Okay then."

And she is out the door.

I watch the sheriff's cruiser back out and head toward the post office. I assume she's going to deliver the mail before she heads down to meet with Edgar and Ceil. I smile. It's so funny when the brand-new summer people see the sheriff sticking her hand into the mailboxes.

Rather than starting the day with too many lies to Mom, I text Ella and tell her to walk my way so we can go to Gusty's. Our biggest goal for the morning is tracking down the sisters, and they are as likely to be at Gusty's, getting an espresso and a cinnamon bun, as they are going to be anywhere else.

* * *

We're lucky to get our table by the window—Gusty's has already filled up. I know Owen Loney would've come and gone already. He's a six-thirty man. But Ms. Stillford might be by the café soon. She usually stops in at a more civilized eight thirty in the summers. No sooner do I think that than she walks through the door.

"Ah, glorious morning, isn't it?" she says.

We nod like bobblehead dolls.

"May I join you, girls?"

"Sure," we both say. Ella lets the smallest groan slip. We'd rather be talking over our plan, but we'd never say no to Ms. Stillford.

Ms. Stillford sits down, hangs her tote bag on the back of the chair, and folds her hands as if she's about to begin meditating. "I know exactly what I'm going to have." She closes her eyes while she recites her order. "Blueberry pancakes, extra thick-cut maple bacon, Vermont maple syrup . . . and a grande latte." Her eyes snap open. "Sound good?"

"Delish," Ella says.

Dad walks up and starts clapping. "A round of applause for the successful completion of eighth grade!" We all clap.

As Dad prepares to take our order, he looks out the window to see Ben and Dominic walking by. "No breakfast for those guys?" Dad asks.

Ella doesn't hesitate. "Ben is teaching Dominic to sail."

"I like to see that," Dad says. "We can always use another sailor around here."

"Dad, have you seen the sisters yet this morning?" I ask.

"Nope. Not yet. They should be in soon though. I set a couple cinnamon buns aside for them."

"How's the espresso machine doing, Gus?" Ms. Stillford asks.

"*Fantastico!*" he says with a Maine version of an Italian accent. "No, really, once I got the hang of it, I was an *experto*." We laugh. "Can I get you a super-caffeinated beverage of your choice, Blythe?"

All this small talk is making me antsy, but what can we do? Nothing, until we locate the sisters.

The café's getting hot. I think Dad should consider turning off the heat, opening the windows, and letting in the fresh air. The overhead fans are windmilling at their regular, tired pace, moving the smell of cinnamon buns around the room. Ms. Stillford starts telling us about her plans for the summer, which include rug hooking, knitting—she's going to dye the wool—and making her own pastels for some studies of the Pidgin Beach lighthouse. I don't tell her that the lighthouse is on my mind too.

A few minutes later, Dad arrives with the food and we all chow down. As we're eating away, I spot something that makes me finish my milk in one gulp: the sisters' van, motoring toward the convent.

"Sorry, Ms. Stillford—are you okay if we leave you here at the table alone?" I say. "We need to go."

"Hmm. Do I detect a bad case of summer vacation fever?"

Ella and I laugh. "I guess you do," I say.

We give her a quick hug and make a break for the door.

## 28

Ella and I jog up to the intersection of Mile Stretch Road and Circle Lane, then hold ourselves steady. We know we won't miss the sisters if we stand right here. If they went to the convent, this intersection's the only way out. If they went into the little town center by Miss Wickham's and the lobster pound, they have to come back this way to leave.

"What are you going to tell them?" Ella asks me.

"I haven't exactly figured that out yet," I say. I'm kind of making this part up as we stand here.

"I can do it," Ella says. "I can tell them."

"Maybe you could sing an Ella Marvell song for them." I'm only half kidding.

She's not kidding when she says, a little crazy-eyed, "Yes. Yes. I'll sing something from *Trouble*."

The long driveway to the convent is quiet. We bounce around by the trash bins near the end. I peek into one of them to see if the new director, Sister Cecelia, is sorting her recycling. She is. Mayor Mom would like that.

Soon I hear the familiar sound of the van engine coming around Circle Lane. Ella knows it too. The sisters were either at the lobster pound or the post office. We position ourselves in the middle of the road, hoping that Sister Ethel is driving and going at her usual snail's pace, rather than Sister Rosie of the Indy 500. They'll come into view any second.

Whew. Sister Ethel is behind the wheel. She sees us and slows down to a crawl. Two nuns wave their arms out the window of the van like the wings of a struggling honeybee.

"Girls!" Sister Rosie says with a big smile on her face. "What's your afternoon like? Do you want to come to the lighthouse? We've got some projects you can work on with the rescue kitties."

I walk to Sister Rosie's passenger-side window while Ella walks to Sister Ethel's driver-side window. We have them surrounded.

"We were just headed to Gusty's," says Sister Ethel.

I want to kick myself. We should have brought them cinnamon buns. I can't think of anything more likely to sway the sisters.

"Sure, Sister," Ella says. "But we need to talk to you first."

A small wrinkle appears between Sister Ethel's eyes, and it isn't caused by her headpiece. "We've been recycling over at the lighthouse, you know."

I can't help myself—I laugh. "No, Sister. It's not about recycling."

Ella leans on the door. "We have a big favor to ask you."

"Well, let's head to the café and you can ask away," says Sister Ethel.

I grab onto the open window frame on Sister Rosie's side. "We need to talk in private."

They look at each other and say at once, "Come on, then. Hop in the van."

The self-regulator voice in my head says, *You are not allowed in that vehicle.* But what we are about to do in the next twelve hours is going to be a way bigger deal than getting in the sisters' van. At least as long as Sister Ethel's driving. So I say okay.

Ella gives me a thank-you look, and in we go.

Sister Ethel points the van toward the cliff above Maiden Rock. When we arrive at the historical marker, she pulls off at the far end, tucks the van behind some trees, and shuts the engine off.

"Now, what's up?" she says.

"Yes, dears. Do tell, do tell," says Sister Rosie.

"Sisters," Ella starts, "we know that you help things in need. You save the cats. And we think that's so . . ."—she searches for a word—"godly."

I add, "We really admire that. I mean, helping save the cats."

Sister Ethel's right eyebrow lifts. "Alright, no need for the wind-up. What's this about?"

Ella's voice trembles. "We need you to help us get my aunt Ceil and uncle Edgar out of town tonight in a boat and take them to the lighthouse so they can sneak away."

The look on the sisters' faces is hard to describe. It morphs from *What?* to *Who?* to *How?* to *Why us?* Finally, Sister Ethel says, "Start again, from the beginning."

The story tumbles out all discombobulated and filled with constant pleas of "and you can't tell anyone."

"So, you want me to take them from the yacht club around to the lighthouse in John Denby's skiff?" Sister Ethel says.

We both nod.

"Tonight?"

We both nod.

"But these are the people who wrote about

kidnapping cats!" cries Sister Rosie.

"Yes, but Sister, the cat was okay in the end. They're good people. It's just a story," I say.

Ella jumps in with something more persuasive: "And they would make a donation to the lighthouse! They would give a lot of money to fix it up and make the clinic better and you could do more neuters."

The sisters slowly turn and look at each other. This is swaying them.

"It would save so many cats," Ella says, "and it would give them a chance to prove they respect the work you're doing."

"I take it your mother does not know about this?" Sister Ethel asks me.

"Edgar and Ceil swore us to secrecy. You'd have to swear too."

Sister Rosie harrumphs. "We don't swear, dears."

"Not like that," Ella says.

Sister Ethel, the more financially savvy of the two, says, "Rosie, all she's saying is that we'd have to keep our peace about it."

"That's all," I say.

"I must tell you, I haven't sailed in years," Sister Ethel says. "Although, in my early days, I could snap a jib as quick as anyone. It's like riding a bike, you know. You never forget."

Ella and I are afraid to show any excitement until we are sure she is agreeing.

"Rosie, you'd have to drive back to the lighthouse from the yacht club without Margaret seeing you."

The thought of getting behind the wheel piques Sister Rosie's interest. "I could do that."

Sister Ethel turns to me and says, "Tell me a little more about Denby's skiff."

# 29

The sisters drop me and Ella off at the yacht club. As I slide the big van door shut, I hear them talking about how they'll spend all the money that Edgar and Ceil are going to donate—the money that Edgar and Ceil have yet to find out that they're donating. That was a stroke of brilliance on Ella's part. As we walk up to the club's doors, Ella wonders out loud how much Edgar and Ceil might be willing to give once they learn about the agreement. I have no doubt they will make a very big contribution.

A small weathered sign hangs crookedly on the door: *Maiden Rock Yacht Club, Founded 1939.* It's not what you would normally think of when you hear the word *yacht.* The club's a big gray barn with a high black roof, white shuttered windows, and double doors that are big enough to wheel a forty foot sailboat through.

I pull at one of the double doors, trusting that Ben has left it unlocked for us. Yes. We slip through and spot a set of open doors at the far end, which leads to the dock.

"This way," I say and lead Ella around to the right, past the six large sailboat hulls hanging in giant straps. Some are dangling mid–paint job, one is missing a keel, another is tipped on its side like it's got an aching bow. We make our way past tools, paint cans, spray bottles, and glass jars filled with black and tarry goo that cover a broken-down work bench.

"Watch out," I tell Ella. "Follow me." I lead her around a disorganized pile of coiled rope. "There they are." I point to Ben, who is in the water with the boat, and Dominic, who is standing on the pier.

"What's Ben doing?" Ella sounds alarmed.

"The boat was anchored in the tidal pool," I tell her. "So he's moved it into a watery parking space."

"Sheesh, why didn't he turn on the motor and drive it here?"

"Oh, no, that would not be the Ben way. Besides, it's more fun to swim-pull it in. It's easy." I run to the boys, take the rope Ben is handing up, and clove-hitch it to the dock.

Ella picks up Ben's dry shirt from the dock and hands it to him as he climbs up.

"Oh, man, the water feels great. I'm itching to take the boat out," he says as he pulls his shirt over his head and rakes his fingers through his hair.

"Will the sisters do it?" Dominic asks.

"They will," I say. "We're set."

"Sister Ethel wants you to text her about the boat, Ben," Ella says.

Dominic hands Ben's phone back to him. Wow—these guys are getting to be actual *friends*.

We sit on the dock as Ben texts Sister Ethel. Ella reads me the deets from over Ben's shoulder: "Seventeen-foot Jersey Skiff, 60 percent sail, 30 percent row, 10 percent motor. Holds four adults. Can be rowed with the mast stepped when the wind dies. Has four-horsepower motor."

It sounds like he's going to go on.

He does: "Originally designed in the mid-1800s for rescue and salvage—"

"Okay, stop," I say. "That's enough for now."

"It's good to have all the information you can about a boat," Ben says. "You never know."

"What's the boat's name?" Ella asks as she walks the length of the boat. "*Connie Will*," she says, reading the stern. "Who is Connie and what *will* she do?"

"Connie and Will," Ben says. "My mom's name

233

was Connie. My dad's name was Will. We named her after my parents."

Ella blushes. I've never seen this before. The girl with confidence galore is horrified by what she said.

She reaches over and takes Ben's hand. "Sorry," Ella says. "I didn't know. Being stupid."

Ben shrugs. "That's okay." Ben lets us all off the hook by saying, "At least we can take her around the pool. We've got plenty of draft."

* * *

You would think that the afternoon before we're about to execute a big plan, we'd be sitting around cross-checking every point, but no. We spend it sailing the *Connie Will* around the tidal pool until we get a little bored and head into the channel and out to sea.

I am not supposed to sail out of the pool without an adult. And I'm pretty sure Ben isn't supposed to take the *Connie Will* out to sea without his uncle, but we're so full of salty air that we motor through the channel to the mighty Atlantic.

We leave the channel and tack northeast. Ben makes lazy eights while the rest of us lean back. We loll out on the boat in the slow rolling waves for an hour, maybe more.

After a while, I notice that everyone's noses have roasted to a peppery red. And I remember the fact that you can catch a sunburn on a cloudy day as easily as on a sunny one. I'm about to point and say, *Hey, you guys are burned, we should go in*, when they look at me and say, "Whoa, Quinnie, you are way burned!"

I touch my face and feel the heat. The breeze has been so steady up to this point, I didn't notice. "We'd better go in," I say.

The sails are taut and we're cutting the water nicely, but Ben agrees with me and steers us to the entrance to the channel, where the wind suddenly whips up and the smooth, rolling water becomes a rough chop. Ben and I ride with it, but Ella grabs the gunwale. Water splashes over us. Dominic's eyes cross as he tries to calm his stomach.

When we're back at the dock, Ben and I secure the boat while Ella and Dominic stagger off. Ella's swallowing like she's trying to steady her stomach. Dominic's taking deep breaths. His skin has the sweaty gloss of nausea.

"What was that? That rough stuff?"

"Will that happen tonight?" Ella wants to know.

"No," I say. "It was a squall. No biggie."

"No biggie," Ben agrees.

Dominic and Ella have to carefully put one foot in front of the other as they walk to the yacht club. But soon we're back to discussing the plan.

"I'll be with Edgar and Ceil, taking the van to the yacht club," Ella says.

"I'll be at the yacht club waiting for you," says Ben.

"But first, we all go see Edgar and Ceil," I say. "Then Dominic and I will go to the café and keep an eye on John and Bob."

By the time we pass Gusty's, the parking lot is full, and that means Dad is serving food like he's on an assembly line. This reduces the chance that he'll see us walking by and ask me to report on where we're going and what we're doing. With every passing house, I begin to gain confidence that we're on the right path.

* * *

When the four of us get to Ella's house, we find Edgar and Ceil drinking depth charges and eating lobster rolls.

"I'm going to miss this food," Edgar says.

"How'd you *get* the food?" Ella asks.

"Oh, your dad went for it," says Ceil. "He's back in his office. He's on fire with this new book."

"Did you tell him?" I ask.

"Oh, no. No. No," says Ceil. "Just going to Bar Harbor for a few days, right, El?"

"No need to mention it, really," Edgar says.

I pick at a few of the cold fries left on the table. There's no buttery lobster dip left in the little paper cup, which is fine, because I think my stomach suffered a little in the squall too.

"Well?" I ask them. "How did it go with Mom this morning?"

Ceil and Edgar glance back and forth and both give up a small shrug.

"I think it went very well," says Ceil.

I look at them like, *a little more detail, please?*

Edgar offers, "She told us about the suspicious activities of the two men and warned us to be cautious and to let her know if we see any worrisome activity."

"Did she ask you if you knew them?" I ask.

Ceil twists her head like she's trying to remember. "Let's see. She asked us if we knew anyone named John Smith or Bob Jones, and she described them as being dressed like fishermen."

"And you said . . ."

"We said we didn't know a John Smith or a Bob Jones who dressed like fishermen."

I feel a pang for Mom. She really wants to help them, and they're not cooperating. I decide not to ask them any more sheriff-related questions. I turn to Ella and mouth, *the donation*, urging her to tell Edgar and Ceil about the commitment she made on the sisters' behalf.

"Aunt Ceil, I have something to tell you."

"What, Ella?" Ceil says. "What is it?"

"When we talked to Sister Rosie and Sister Ethel . . ."

Ella's struggling. I want to jump in and help, but I know it will be better if this comes from her. "And we wanted them to be very comfortable. No, we wanted them to be enthusiastic. No, not that either. We wanted them to feel like helping would be a really good thing."

Edgar's face turns stony. "What's wrong? Don't they want to do it?"

"No. No. I mean yes. They do want to do it. It's just that we wanted them to know that you cared about their cause, just like they care about helping you."

"Is there a *but* in this story?" asks Ceil.

"Not a *but*. An *and*." Ella bites her green nail. "And we said you . . . I said . . . you would make a contribution to the cat-rescue lighthouse." She takes a deep breath and holds it.

"Oh, for heaven's sake." Ceil laughs. "I thought it was something serious. Of course we'll make a contribution to their cause."

"How much should we give them?" Edgar takes out his wallet and pulls out a wad of cash. "One hundred? Two hundred. I have four hundred in cash right here. Take it."

"I think, maybe, they think it will be more." Ella's voice is as small and squeaky as a cartoon mouse.

"How much more, Ella?" Ceil says.

We never gave the sisters an actual number, but we did talk about renovations to the lighthouse. They have every reason to believe it would be thousands.

Ella clears her throat. "Err, uh. Fifty thousand dollars." She looks to me for support.

"Yes," I say. "They would be thrilled if you made a donation, or contribution, or whatever, of that much."

"To a cat rescue organization in Maiden Rock, Maine?" says Edgar, his voice leaping an octave.

Ben pipes up: "Actually, it's in Pidgin Beach." I give him a look and he shrinks back.

"Edgar, I don't care if it's on the moon. Let's donate whatever they need to get their little place in shape. I'm fine with that—whatever it takes," says Ceil.

"*Great*," says Edgar sarcastically, "that's just what the world needs, a lighthouse full of spoiled cats."

"Shut up, Edgar," Ceil says. Edgar closes his mouth.

Done. For fifty thousand dollars, they get a nighttime cruise from Maiden Rock to Pidgin Beach in the *Connie Will*, and if there's a squall—and they still get there safely—that's a very fair price.

Ella hugs Ceil, then squeezes Edgar around the waist until he groans for relief.

I check the nearest clock. It's time for Dominic and me to go to the café and pretend to eat. Ben goes with us so his uncle will have a chance to see him. That way, John Denby won't be wondering where he is. From there, he'll head to the yacht club.

My gut is still churning when we leave the Philpotts' place. I hug Ceil and Edgar. I even hug Ella. I can't tell if my stomach is roiling from anticipation or if it's still a little squall-sick.

## 30

By the time we reach Gusty's, some of the dinner-rush cars have cleared out. It's warm and cheery inside. Ben goes over to talk to his uncle, who's at the counter with his big hands wrapped around a coffee mug. Clooney is behind the counter talking to Dad. She'll be taking over for the evening now.

We sit at our table, waiting while Dad circles the room with a coffeepot. When he reaches us, the first thing he says is, "Looks like you guys got some sun out there."

Dominic pours out how much fun he had sailing around the Pool, smiling through his lingering queasiness, and Dad seems perfectly satisfied. "Good thing you didn't get caught in that squall. We got clobbered here for a bit."

We say nothing.

"So? What's it gonna be?"

I'm not hungry, but I know I have to order something. Chowder? No, too thick. Lobster roll? No, too creamy and chunky. Gusty burger? Too meaty, but I could eat the English muffin it comes on. Crab cake? No, too spicy. Cream of Wheat? That might be okay.

"Cream of Wheat."

He looks at me like I'm sick or something. "Cream of Wheat? For dinner?"

"Just have a taste for it."

"Okay then. I'll fix it up nice for you, with some blueberries and brown sugar."

"Okay, Dad. Thanks."

Dominic is struggling with the same problem. He's smart, though. "I'll try some of that Cream of Wheat, but I'll have the blueberries and brown sugar on the side."

Dad's getting into it. "You know, I could mix some sour cream with the brown sugar and add a smidge of maple syrup, like a fruit sauce."

"Great," Dominic says weakly. "Just on the side, please."

"If you really like it, I might put it in the menu!" Dad says.

After chatting with his uncle, Ben walks up and pulls out a chair, while I look out the window for John and Bob. Nothing yet.

Ben has come back to the table in time for Clooney to serve up his Gusty burger, fries, chowder, milk, and two whoopie pies. She sets his order down with an approving smile. We, on the other hand, get the kind of look from her that usually comes with a head scratch.

"Never seen that b'fore."

I taste my Cream of Wheat, and it's just perfect. Ben is wolfing his burger. I reach for my phone to check the time and realize I left it on my desk—next to the note I wrote Mom. So not only do I not have my phone with me, I didn't put the note where she could find it later. Great.

Dominic sees me patting my pockets and says, "It's okay. I've got my phone if we need it."

"What time is it?" Ben asks.

"Quarter to seven," Dominic answers.

Ben drains his glass of milk and squishes the last half of whoopie pie into his mouth. "I gotta get to the yacht club. I told my uncle that I was cleaning the boat and I planned to show you around it, Dom."

Dom? I would never have taken Dominic for a *Dom*. I guess he's cool with it, coming from Ben, but I make a mental note never to use the nickname. It just doesn't fit—for me.

Ben's out the door at the same time John and Bob come in. They're in full-on L.L.Bean wear again. Boy, those clothes must smell pretty bad. Don't people notice this? I guess not. Everyone is smiling at them and slapping them on the back, and they're playing it up.

I must have stared at them too long, because John turns and catches my eye, and his big fat smile fades. I get flustered and drop my spoon into my Cream of Wheat. A white glob splats on the table.

"Hang on to the hot cereal," Dominic says, but when he follows my gaze to John, his spoon rattles his dish too. He starts tugging at my sleeve. "Maybe we should go."

I glance nervously out the window, and at that instant, the sisters' van drives by, headed for the yacht club. Little do the other diners know that Edgar and Ceil are on the first leg of their escape.

"No," I whisper to Dominic. "Our job is to watch these guys and let Ben know if they leave the café."

Dominic doesn't like this answer, but we stay where we are, pushing the Cream of Wheat around our bowls. We steal peeks at the John and Bob table. We watch the sky go from blue to pink to gray, and lights snap on in beach houses across the street.

Edgar and Ceil must be in the boat by now, I think, but Sister Rosie hasn't driven back this way. I want Dominic to call Ben, but he doesn't want to use the phone while we're here in the café. He's become very skittish about old John and Bob. I make him at least text. Ben doesn't reply.

It's not my imagination. John keeps looking at me. At least every other time I check, he's got me in his gaze.

I feel a growing urge to get out of the café and get to the yacht club to be sure everything is fine. "Okay. I think we should go."

As we get up to leave, I catch Mom's cruiser pulling into the parking lot. She's back from Rook River. Crossing paths with us at the café entrance, she asks me, "Where are you kids headed?"

Always with the questions! But I'm ready for this one. "We're walking up to the yacht club to watch Ben clean the boat."

I follow the Detective Monroe Spalding rule I learned last fall: The cleverest lie is the one that is closest to the truth.

Mom assesses the fading light outside. "Well, that can't go on too long. Don't be late. I'm heading home in a minute."

I feel a little bit terrible as she gives me a good-bye

hug, but not terrible enough to call this all off or betray Edgar and Ceil's confidence.

After putting a few steps between us and the café, we can see small figures moving on the yacht club dock. They're visible in that hazy half-light between day and night. It's not high tide anymore, but it's still two hours to low tide. They have plenty of time to get out of the channel before the water is so low the boat will get stuck in the sandy mud. They just need to get going.

We're fifty feet away from Gusty's when we hear the café door open and a group of people crowd out. I look over my shoulder. One of them is Mom. Two of them are John and Bob.

Dominic has his arm around my waist now, and I have my arm around his. We pick up our pace, pulling each other forward. Move. Move. We're nearing the end of Mile Stretch Road, where we'll turn left on Circle Lane, when headlights flood over us.

We don't check over our shoulders. We just keep walking.

The car behind us slows to keep our pace. Then the passenger window powers down.

"Hey, you kids." It's John. I haven't truly heard his voice before. It's gravely. "You wanna ride somewhere? Where ya going? It's getting dark out here."

"No, thank you," Dominic says without turning to look at him.

We're only feet from the yacht club. If they don't pull away, they'll know exactly where we're going because we'll be there.

They don't pull away. I veer to the right, taking Dominic with me, and cross in front of their car, toward the Lobster Pound. The car continues following us—past Miss Wickham's, the Bradfords' tiny grocery store, the post office. At the next turn, before John and Bob's car rounds the bend, I grab Dominic's hand and pull him into the dense bushes around Circle Lane. We crouch down as their beams appear on the lane, flooding it with light. The car stops, but the engine keeps running.

"Just stay still," I tell Dominic. "They'll probably think we went into Miss Wickham's."

A minute passes before the car backs up and then noses into a parking spot in front of the B&B. Once they're inside, I move—"Now!"

Dominic and I turn into the deeper brush and thrash through to the other side, coming out across from the yacht club. Five seconds later, we are behind the club's big doors. It looks entirely different at night. A single barn light at the top of the roof ridge shines down on the hanging boat hulls, making them look like monstrous bats in Count Dracula's crypt. I can hear Sister Ethel out on the dock, telling Edgar where to stow his bag.

We feel our way through the building, toward the dock, and see Edgar and Ceil finding their places in the *Connie Will*'s rocking hull. Sister Ethel is poised on the bow, wearing cargo pants, boat shoes, a sweatshirt, and her veil. Ben is untying the spring line, while Ella hangs over the edge of the dock, trying to touch hands with Ceil.

Sister Ethel tells Ben to cast them off. He does.

But the second the *Connie Will* pushes away from the dock, Ella takes a flying leap and lands between Edgar and Ceil, nearly capsizing the boat.

# 31

I run onto the dock and whisper-bark, "Ella, get out of the boat!"

She links arms with Ceil instead.

I turn to Sister Ethel for support, but she says, "I think it's fine, Quinnie. She's where she wants to be."

I'm kind of trapped. I don't like this rearranging of our reasonable plans, but there's not much I can do about it. And to be honest, Ella is planted in that boat like nothing will get her out. And they need to get going.

"Right."

I guess I'll see Ella when she's back from the lighthouse.

Sister Ethel slowly angles the *Connie Will* away from the dock and into the waters of the Pool. Dominic and I head back to the boathouse, leaving Ben to do some rope-wrapping at the dock. We've barely stepped inside when we hear the creak of the large front doors.

Ben slips over the dock's edge into the water, while Dominic and I creep around one of the hanging hulls and hold our breath.

Bob's deep voice fills the yacht club. "Ohhh Victoria? Victoria Kensington? We know you guys are in here."

"All we want's our money," John yells. "Just what the Count says you owe us."

Their footsteps plod in our direction, and we tuck ourselves into the shadow under a boat hull.

The light from above illuminates Bob, digging through tools at the workbench. He picks up a pipe wrench the size of a hatchet and tests its balance in his hand. "Yeah. Hey, Lardy, this will do."

*Lardy?* Who the heck is Lardy? John? How many names do these guys have?

Lardy moves around the boats, pushing on them and making them sway in place. "Just tell us where Gordo hid the loot and everything will be good. We don't want to hurt you." He's talking to Ceil and Edgar again, or trying to. "But we can do it that way, if that's the way you want it."

My brain is going *zzt-zzt-zzt*. Who's *Gordo*? Their share of the *loot*? What loot? *Wait. A. Maine Minute.*

These guys aren't crazy fans. These guys are crooks.

"We know you know where the money is, so come on out now," Lardy yells. "Look over there, Snooks."

*Snooks?* Really? Bob is Snooks? Snooks Jones?

"Yeah," says Snooks.

Snooks is good at saying "Yeah." His tan pants and newish Top-Siders move within feet of us, and we see the tip of the pipe wrench. Luckily, he's either too stupid or too lazy to bend down.

"It's no use," yells Lardy. "We know that you know. You wouldn't 'a' had any idea about that damn cat in the van if Gordo hadn't told ya."

"Yeah," says Snooks. "You and Gordo were prob'ly laughing yourselves sick about us being stuck in there with that evil cat, but you're not laughin' now, are ya? You're gonna wish you never heard about the bank job, let alone put it in your stupid book."

Dominic's forehead has wrinkled upward. He's putting this mess together at the same time I am. His eyes scream, *Are you getting this?*

I nod and push on his hand. *Stay quiet.*

But the silence breaks when all the boats at the dock start bumping together. Ben must be trying to crawl up onto the dock. But why's he doing *that*?

"Out there," Lardy yells to Snooks. "They're gettin' away! In a boat!"

Lardy runs to the dock with Snooks behind him, hauling the heavy pipe wrench. Ben dives back in the water, next to a boat.

"I'll get a boat," Lardy says. "You get that kid in the water!"

Snooks runs up and down the dock, alternately looking for Ben and looking at the heavy wrench in his hand.

Lardy boards an old yacht club motorboat that always has the keys in it. He turns over the motor and screams, "Snooks! Come on! They're gettin' away!"

Snooks is all too happy to hurl the heavy wrench into the water at Ben and climb into the boat with Lardy.

I almost yell, *Oh, no, Ben!* as the heavy thing splashes into the water next to him and he darts under the dock.

Lardy and Snooks have a tangled time trying to cast off, but soon they're cutting through the Pool waters at a speed that could easily overtake the *Connie Will*.

Dominic and I rush to the dock, yelling, "Ben! Ben!"

Ben pops up amid a throng of boats banging around from the wake.

There's no time to be relieved that he's okay. "Pick a boat," I yell. "We have to follow them!"

In a split second, Ben's aboard the Morgan family's little ten-foot Navigator.

"A training boat? Really?" I yell.

"It's this or nothing," he yells back.

The next thing I know, all three of us are aboard. Ben has started the motor. I'm hoisting the sails, and Dominic is looking everywhere for a life preserver.

As we come around the lobster pound, headed into the channel, I see something that would've been bad news an hour ago but now makes me feel nothing but relief: Mom's cruiser has screamed up with its sirens and flashers in hot pursuit mode. The trouble is, it's headed for the lobster pound, not the yacht club. What the heck is she doing?

# 32

The tide is going out fast and taking me, Ben, and Dominic onto the open sea. We're riding low in the water, and waves are splashing over us each time our bow cuts into a swell. But at the spot where the narrow outlet from the channel meets the Atlantic currents, we hit slack water and stall. Dominic crouches as low as he can, trying to stay out of the way as Ben and I urge the boat to go south. The little tiny motor is straining, and the wind at our backs is feeble.

I think, Okay, this is a good time to call Mom. Except when I pat my pockets, I remember I left my phone at home. I ask Dominic for his, and he leans to the side so I can reach into his pocket. No point. Dominic's phone has zero bars. I want to throw it overboard, but I jam it back in his pocket.

Ben has pulled up a paddle from the bottom of the boat and handed it to Dominic.

"Stroke, stroke," he says to him and points south.

Maybe two hundred feet ahead of us, Lardy and Snooks's motorboat has stalled out and started rolling in the waves, its onboard lights bobbing up and down. We're coming up on them, slowly. They're arguing and yanking at the pull cord on the motor. Beyond both our boats, the fog is rolling in.

"Go around them, go around them," I keep saying to Ben, who is holding the rudder and the main sail. Salt spray has soaked my hair through to my scalp.

"Give me more speed," he says, but the Morgan family's little putt-putt engine is full out, and I'm afraid it will blow.

We have no running lights, so Lardy and Snooks do not see us laboring toward them. And they're yelling so much about engine trouble that they don't hear us coming. To keep it that way, Ben cuts our engine, and our momentum takes us port side of them. For a few seconds, we're sailing by close enough that they could reach out and grab us, but they don't realize it, and a swell lifts us right past them.

"What the—!?" Lardy screams when he finally sees us. "Get them!" he yells to Snooks. "Grab that boat."

Snooks looks around like he doesn't know what Lardy is talking about. He missed our float-by entirely.

When Lardy points in our direction, Dominic raises his hand and waves at them.

Lardy starts cussing a streak as we charge south using wind power and a little paddle power.

A foghorn blasts in the distance. It's telling us to get to shore.

Through the rising and falling waves, I think I see the *Connie Will* ahead of us. Her one running light bobs up, then disappears. We're up, I see it. We're down, I don't. They're up, I see it. They're down, I don't. The swells underneath us seem to be getting bigger, and the wall of whispery gray fog that was a mile away a minute ago has now blotted out the moon.

"I see them," Ben says.

"Are you sure?" I ask. I'm questioning which way is which, until I catch a glimpse of lights from the beach houses. Thank goodness. We're still headed south.

"Oh, man. I just heard a motor start up behind us," Dominic says, paddling faster. "Hurry! Those guys'll be on us soon."

The fog is on my skin. In my hair. Up my nose. I'm starting to think we should beach the boat while we can still see the houses along the coast. We could be right in front of *my* house, for all I know. I want to tell Sister Ethel to beach the *Connie Will*, too, and run for it. Run up to my house. Don't go around the point. Don't risk the rocks.

Where is Mom, I wonder? What was she doing at the pound? Is she back at home? I wish I was back at home. I wish we were all back at home.

The *vroom* of a motorboat closes in on us. I pray they don't hit us. They don't. But Lardy and Snooks come so close, their wake rocks our boat violently. We see only the stern as they speed past us, bearing down on the *Connie Will*.

Ella and Sister Ethel have no idea what Lardy and Snooks really want. And Lardy and Snooks have no idea that, in addition to Edgar and Ceil, there's a nun and a young girl onboard the *Connie Will*.

Dominic stops rowing and fumbles in his pocket. "How do you do SOS on a cell phone?"

"It's no good," I tell him. "I tried."

"No signal. No signal. No flipping signal." He waves his phone in the air.

Through the fog, I hear Sister Ethel yelling, "You'll never board us!"

Then Ella screams, "Help!"

## 33

I hear the thud of hulls banging together. We reach the scene seconds later. The other two boats are bumping and knocking, and the wake from the tussle sends us in the opposite direction. Ben and I drop to our knees and start stroking the water with our arms, trying to draw ourselves toward the *Connie Will*, as a mouthful of salt water burns through to my nose.

"What the—?" Lardy's voice fills the night. "Who are they?"

I have to get there. I have to try and save them. I have no idea what I'll do, but I'll do something!

Like he's reading my mind, Dominic offers me his paddle. I reach up to grab it, but when he stands to give it to me, our boat rocks violently, and I twist and fall backward overboard.

"Quinnie!" Ben yells.

Dominic is trying to get out of the way, but he steps backward to do it. This rocks our boat again, catching Ben off guard. In a blink, he loses his footing and falls overboard in the other direction.

Now I'm freaking out. Freezing and freaking out. Ben and I are desperately treading water, while Sister Ethel's yelling "Back off, you creeps!" in the distance. Dominic has crouched down, holding onto the gunwale of our boat, which the tide is tugging out to sea.

"Where's the paddle!?" I yell to Dominic.

He points overboard, then, as if he realizes what a big problem that is, he starts to paddle the water with his hands, feverishly digging into the waves. But it's a useless effort.

"Get your hands off me!" Ella's voice rings out again.

Ben starts to swim toward her.

"No! Ben, go for Dominic," I yell. "You're the strongest swimmer!"

Dominic is a helpless passenger. If we don't catch him right now, he'll disappear behind the curtain of gray fog. Ben shifts his attention and puts all his swimming power into catching up with the Morgans' boat.

I turn and attack the waves between the *Connie Will* and me.

"Ella!" Ceil screams.

"Aunt Ceil!" Ella cries out, followed by a splash.

"Get her, Edgar!" Ceil says.

Behind the fog, the voices seem to be coming from different directions. I swim toward the sound of Ella's voice.

"Edgar! Help!" Ceil yells, followed by a splash. Now she's in the water too.

I reach the *Connie Will* and cling onto the side, pulling myself up to see what's happening.

Sister Ethel is struggling with Snooks, who's trying to toss her overboard. The fierce nun looks like she's winning.

Lardy pulls at Edgar's shoulders while Edgar hangs over the stern, trying to hoist Ceil back aboard. Ceil's left arm is dangling at a crazy angle and she's whimpering. Ella is behind her in the chilly water, trying to hang onto her aunt.

The cold is getting to me. My teeth are starting to chatter. I'm not sure whether I should climb aboard to help pull Ceil in or swim around to Ella.

Through the mist, I hear Ben yelling to Dominic and Dominic yelling back.

Suddenly, Ceil cries out in agony as Edgar strains to pull her up.

I make my way around the boat as fast as I can,

intending to help Ella.

Sister Ethel keeps banging her fists on Snooks's head and shouting, "You swine!"

Up close, I see Edgar's in a rage trying to free himself from Lardy. He finally bites into the crook's forearm.

Lardy yelps, spins Edgar around, and screams, "No more games! Where's the loot? We want our share!"

Edgar tilts his head like he's trying to understand. "Loot? We don't have any loot."

"Don't give me that," growls Lardy. "You wrote all about it in that book."

I take this opportunity to boost Ella aboard the boat, then wrap my arms around its gunwale.

"The book," Ceil whimpers. "The diner! The story!"

"What diner?" Lardy demands to know. "Is it stashed at a diner!?"

A look somewhere between fear and embarrassment passes across Edgar's face. He understands . . . something. "Help me get her in the boat and I'll tell you everything," he pleads.

"You'll tell me now or she ain't gettin' in this boat ever again," Lardy says.

"Tell him, Edgar," Ceil begs.

Snooks lets go of Sister Ethel and turns to hear what Edgar's going to say. The ocean seems to freeze in place.

"We didn't steal your money," Edgar says. "We stole your story."

# 34

"What're you talkin' about?" Lardy screams. "We ain't got a story! You write the stories."

I look at Lardy, who's looking at Edgar, who's looking at Ceil who is cradling her arm and wincing.

And the roar of a boat engine fills my ears.

A big, big boat from the sound of it. Whatever it is, if it doesn't see us in this murk, it could plow us right over. I start screaming, "Stop! Stop!" Everyone else realizes why I'm doing this and joins in—even Lardy and Snooks. "Stop! Stop! Stop!"

The engine roar cuts back to an idle. Whoever's driving has tried to bring the craft to a halt. Still, I know the momentum may force it straight through us before we can be seen. I look for the right direction to dive off, just in case. Suddenly, two large boats appear. The *Blythe Spirit*, Owen Loney's trusty lobster boat, pierces the fog barrier. It sidles in next to us with Loney at the helm and Mom leaning over the side. A huge white Coast Guard cutter looms behind them.

"This is the Coast Guard," a woman's voice yells over a bullhorn. "Stay where you are until we pick you up. Stay where you are until we pick you up."

A crisscross of brilliant light beams sweeps the area and slices through the fog. Ceil and Edgar's escape boat bangs against the cutter's hull.

We're boxed in. Lardy and Snooks sink down to the floor, resigned to the fact that they're trapped. I shout to Mom, "Dominic and Ben are still out there without a paddle!"

"We're here!" I hear Ben yell.

Mom runs to the starboard side of the *Blythe Spirit* and calls into the fog, "This way! Follow my voice, boys! Keep it coming straight this way!" She grabs a gaff hook and leans over to turn and steady them as they plow into the side of the lobster boat.

As the captain of the cutter is barking orders to her crew, I yell up to them, "Ceil hurt her arm. We're cold. We need blankets."

"We're coming aboard," a man calls back.

I sit down and hold on.

* * *

Mom boards the *Connie Will* first, pointing out Lardy and Snooks to the Coast Guard. Next, she helps Ceil onto a stretcher that a Coast Guard medic has lowered down and directs me, Edgar, Sister Ethel, and Ella to climb up the ladder to the cutter's deck. I ask where Dominic and Ben are, and she tells me they're already on board the *Blythe Spirit*.

It's a fast and choppy cutter ride to the Rook River harbor, where harsh lights and lots of people are waiting to meet us. Emerging from a cocoon of blankets, I see the *Blythe Spirit* next to us at the dock.

A paramedic guides me down the cutter's gangplank, trailing Ella and Sister Ethel, and I step into one of the ambulances. Another paramedic helps Ceil and Edgar in with me. The paramedics keep trying to keep Ceil flat on the stretcher, but she won't stay still. She moans and grabs her arm. Edgar is whiter than I've ever seen him. Finally, one of the paramedics grabs a splint and wraps Ceil's left arm, the one she hurt when she went overboard. The other paramedic jabs an IV in her right arm, and a bag of something starts flowing. It must be a painkiller, since she falls back on the stretcher and relaxes almost immediately.

## 35

I'm face-to-face with Dad in the Rook River Hospital Emergency Room, and I can tell that he has worried his brain to a crisp. He grabs me and squeezes me so hard I wince. Before I know what's happening, he has his arm around me, and I'm up and moving. We push our way past nurses and doctors, from one curtained space to another, looking for Mom. We finally find her talking to a Coast Guard officer and making notes. We wait for her to turn our way.

Mom says the hospital is holding Ceil overnight for observation, and Edgar is staying with her. Ella wants to stay too, but her dad is making her go home with him. Like me, she had a close call with hypothermia, but the doctors say we'll be okay.

As Dad drives me and Mom home, Mom tells me that she's arranged an interview with the sisters first thing tomorrow morning. I can tell she's still a little suspicious of the idea that Rosie and Ethel were actually helping this time around. Once I straggle into the house, before I go to my room, I say to Mom, "What happened to John and Bob? I mean, Lardy and Snooks. The guys, with the . . ."

"They're in custody in Rook River."

# 36

The next day, Edgar and Ceil come to our house to be interviewed. I take this as a good sign. At least they're cooperating with Mom.

Normally, Mom would interview witnesses behind the door of her small, multi-purpose home office, but this thing has gotten way too big, what with the mysterious John and Bob and a high speed chase on the ocean. The captain of the Coast Guard cutter is here. An FBI guy is here. It's all happening in our dining room.

Before it starts, I try to talk to Mom. "I have something to tell you," I say. I want her to know this whole thing is somehow about stolen stories.

"Later, Quinnette," she says. Her voice isn't what I'd call angry. It's more like her I'm-so-disappointed-that-I-can't-talk-to-you-right-now voice. I've heard it once before. I feel terrible.

But not so terrible that Ella and I don't eavesdrop on the interview. Ben and Dominic are in lockdown, grounded, so they can't be here. But Ella and I position ourselves at the top of the stairs and compare bruises until it starts.

"I'm going to tape this to be sure we get it all," Mom says.

"Fine, fine," Edgar says.

"Okay. Let's begin. In your own words, tell us when this all started."

"We write a series of vampire novels about a Count Le Plasma, and as part of the—uh—charm of the series, we profess to be in direct communication with the Count," Edgar says.

"He tells us his stories, and we write them down," says Ceil.

"But," says Mom, "you don't actually talk to vampires." It's not a question. It's a statement of fact.

"Correct," says Edgar.

"And we have some unusual fans who are infatuated with vampires," says Ceil.

"Two of them have been following us, claiming that they talk to the Count too and that he's told them they can have the profits from our most recent book," says Edgar.

"And they've been stalking us, demanding the money," says Ceil.

Edgar clears his throat and then goes on. "And we thought that was all this was about. Simple, out-of-control vampire worship."

Ella and I scoot to the edge of the step we're sitting on, waiting for Edgar to explain what he blurted out at Lardy in the boat.

"Jack and Wally Woodley—" Edgar starts.

"Ah, you mean Edward Regan and Donald Fisher," says the FBI man. "Go on."

"Anyhow," Edgar says, "a little over two years ago"—he stops and coughs—"we were at our regular haunt on Fifth in Park Slope, drinking double espressos and brainstorming our next book, and two churlish sorts were seated at the next table over."

"We weren't paying attention to them at first, but then we heard them grumbling and getting themselves pretty worked up about something," says Ceil.

"We weren't eavesdropping," says Edgar. "But they grew more and more upset over someone named Gordo. For running off with *the loot*."

"Our first reaction was, let's get out of here. But then they started to talk about the cat," says Ceil. "It was a gem of a story! They kidnapped a bank guard's prize cat and swore they'd hold it hostage until the guard unlocked the safe for them. And the poor man was so distraught, he did whatever they wanted."

"And this is the best part: they described being in a van with the cat. They'd been stationed inside while their"—Edgar searches for the word—"*colleague* did the robbing. Many hours in a van with the cat and its terrible temper and litter box. Meanwhile, this Gordo got the money and took off."

Ella and I look at each other and at the same time mouth the words, *Transylvanian Drip!*

It all comes together. Edgar and Ceil used the story they overheard for their book . . . and when Lardy and Snooks read the book . . . they thought Edgar and Ceil were in on the heist.

"Like the Count bailing on his assistants!" cries the FBI man.

"Yes," says Edgar. "We used the *premise* in our latest book."

"But with a blood bank!" The FBI man sounds delighted with himself for figuring this out.

"The trouble came when we went on *Celebrity Dish with Buddy Denton* and revealed that we were the authors behind Victoria Kensington," says Ceil. "Apparently, these thugs saw the show and heard us talking about a heist involving a cat–napping and, well, they must have thought that we were in league with this Gordo person. Silent partners, embezzlers—I don't know."

"That's when we started getting the notes."

Mom's more interested in the real crime: "Did you hear anything about where Gordo might have gone or where they had planned to meet him?"

"Sure," says Ceil. "*Gordo* was in prison upstate. They were trying to figure out where he'd hidden the loot."

"What did the letters say?" the FBI agent asks. "Do you still have them?"

"Oh, yes," says Edgar.

"It was funny at first. Then it became frightening, then terrifying," says Ceil.

It's not funny, but I want to giggle in relief. Truth is stranger than fiction.

Mom and the FBI man excuse themselves and step outside, leaving the Coast Guard officer to sit with the authors. Ella and I watch them talking intensely for a few minutes before they go back in.

Mom says to Edgar and Ceil, "To be clear, you *do not* personally associate with this Gordo?"

Edgar and Ceil laugh. "No!" they say together. "We don't know anyone named Gordo. And we don't know where any *loot* is."

Ceil continues: "And we wish like heaven that we'd used the other idea we had. The story begins in Monte Carlo, where a gambler has been plotting to steal the Count's gold . . ."

# 37

This is the second time that I have had to have a super-serious sit-down with my parents while they're struggling not to pull their hair out. The first was last autumn, after the whole Ms. Stillford thing. Once again, I am contrite. Really! But the *once again* part makes things awkward.

"I don't understand why you can't stop yourself from jumping into risky situations."

"I can't explain it either."

"This whole high seas episode might not have happened if you had just told me what Ceil and Edgar told you."

"They wouldn't let me, Mom. I tried."

"It should not have been their choice, Quinnette. Not entirely. Other people were in danger."

"And if I hadn't tried to help them, they could have been captured by Lardy and Snooks and be dead now."

I can tell that even Mom wants to concede that last part's true. Still, I admit I could have done a couple things differently. Mom says it's hard to help people who don't want help.

Dad says he'll make a deal with me: if I stay out of detective trouble until I'm fifteen, I can work at Gusty's as a hostess starting on that birthday. Though even then, he says, I don't get to operate the espresso maker. It's too dangerous. I think he's exaggerating, but I don't argue. This is progress.

## 38

"I can't believe they're leaving tomorrow," Ella says.

She's hanging out on my back porch with me, Dominic, and Ben, watching the waves—and the arrival of the newest crop of summer people—and waiting for my mom to do something she promised to do. Poor summer people, they have no idea that a pair of bank robbers stalked this little strip of beach a mere week ago.

While Ella dangles her feet (adorned with Coral Ember Fire toenail polish) over the railing, I practice tossing Dominic's new hat on his head. He's kindly ducking, bobbing, and swaying to make my efforts more successful. Ben is eating an entire bag of Oreos, even though we're meeting Edgar and Ceil at Gusty's for a good-bye lunch in less than an hour.

"Hey, look." Ella points to a lanky boy in shorts and a soccer jersey; he's kicking sand at someone who must be his little sister. "I bet he's fourteen."

"Agree," I say, then motion up the beach. "How old do you think she is?"

"Oh, fifteen, easy," Ella says.

Dominic and Ben stand up as the girl with short, curly red hair begins talking to the boy in the shorts.

Mom opens the door behind us and says, "Ready?"

I take a deep breath. "*Are* we ready?" I ask my friends.

They practically run me over on the way to Mom's office.

"I guess they're ready," I tell Mom.

Rescue footage, here we come.

Mom slips into her sheriff's chair and tilts her computer screen so we can all see it. Ella claps.

"Don't celebrate yet," Mom says and laughs. "It's not exactly an Academy Award–winning production."

She clicks a few times, and a recording springs to life. It's me, the day Mom first got her body cam. I'm squealing and covering my face while Mom calls after me, *I'm watching you.*

Mom fast-forwards through hours of boring shoulder-cam viewing. "Let me see where we are," she says, halting the fast-forward and hitting play. We all stare at the screen and squint. Onscreen Mom is running through bushes and trees in the dark with a flashlight. Then we hear Ben's uncle John: *Over here, Margaret.*

Mom pauses the video and then presses fast-forward again.

"Stop. Stop," we all yell at Mom. "Go back. What was that?"

"Nothing," she says. "A night in the life of a sheriff."

"Mom, please." I tug at her shoulder. "Why were you running in the woods?"

"Oh, man, were you and my uncle chasing the coyote?" Ben asks.

"Can we see it?" Dominic adds.

Mom reverses the video to the point of her running in the woods. "It's a little heart-wrenching," she says.

The four of us crowd together to watch from the Mom's-eye view as she thrashes through brush, crashes past trees, and cuts a zigzag path through Becker's Woods—all the time calling back and forth with John Denby, whose flashlight beam is cutting in front of her at crazy angles.

*Over here, Margaret*, yells John Denby. *I think I hit something.*

Mom pushes through branches.

*Here*, John Denby says from somewhere in the dark.

*Coming*, Mom calls back.

Crash, crash, smash. Heavy breathing.

The flashlights of Mom and John Denby come together to create a pool of brightness over a full-grown coyote lying on its side, breathing heavily.

*Here*, John Denby says. He waves his rifle. *Looks like I nicked her ear.*

*Look, look!* Mom angles her light. Near the coyote are five little pups. *She's a mama.*

"What happened?" Ella asks Mom. "Is she okay? Are they okay?"

"They're all fine," Mom says. "We took them to the cat rescue. The sisters're nursing the mama's ear and finding a home for them all at a nature preserve."

"Keep going, okay?" Ben says. "I mean, please keep going, Mrs. Boyd."

That Ben. He's a softy down deep.

Mom fast-forwards again. Now we're getting to the night of nights. She stops at a scene in Gusty's: she's positioned herself so that she can record John and Bob alone at a table. The John and Bob she's recording are not bumbling, jolly, chowder-loving jokers. They don't seem to realize they're being watched, so they slip into rougher postures, jowlier expressions, and occasional sneers when a Mainah walks by.

"You've been watching them?" asks Dominic.

"I've been watching them," says Mom.

"How long?" I ask.

"For a while," she says.

She fast-forwards to a whole series of clips of John and Bob: on the beach, driving around, going into the B&B, stopped by Mom for *going a little too fast*.

"You've *really* been watching them."

"Indeed."

I'm starting to realize that Mom was curious about John and Bob before I was.

The next clip is the one we've all been waiting for. Mom's patrol car races up to Loney's Lobster Pound. She jumps out and runs inside to where Owen Loney is hosing down lobster tanks.

*Owen, fire up the* Blythe Spirit. *We're on a mission!*

Without asking a question, he turns off the hose, pulls off his big rubber apron, and heads to the boat. A few minutes later, the boat lurches up and down, headed into the channel.

Mom is on the radio SOS-ing the Coast Guard with locations and descriptions of two dangerous characters. The *Blythe Spirit*'s radio crackles and a voice comes through. *Broadcast your position*, Blythe Spirit, *cutter is on the way.*

Mom's body-cam footage is dark and noisy for several minutes. Water beads splash on the lens as

Mom rolls and pitches with the boat. Suddenly, two small craft come into view. We faintly hear Dominic and Ben, then Mom's arms pulling them onto the *Blythe Spirit*. The Coast Guard cutter looms into the camera's frame, dwarfing the lobster boat and casting a massive shadow. "Over here! Easy as you go!" Mom calls. "Small craft ahead." The cutter's searchlights pierce the sky, one of them blasting directly into the camera's lens. A brilliant white fills Mom's computer screen—*Hey!*

Mom shuts off the footage.

Dominic groans. "I thought I was going to visit that friend of yours in Scotland, Quinnie."

"I thought you were going to visit some lobsters in their natural habitat," says Ben.

"That was scary," I say.

"It was," Mom says.

"I'm sorry," I say.

"I know," she says.

"It was horrible," says Ella.

"I agree with that too," Mom says, "and now it's evidence against the L.L.Bean boys, just like the statements you gave the FBI." She shuts off the computer and pushes away from her desk. "Okay, my young, incorrigible detectives—let's go to Gusty's and enjoy this time with Edgar and Ceil."

* * *

"You guys are lucky," Dominic says to the rest of us while we take Mile Stretch Road toward Gusty's.

"Why's that?" I ask.

"My parents were so mad about our Edgar and Ceil escape plan, they threatened to end our time in Maiden Rock early and take me away from this craziness."

"Aww, we aren't that lucky." Ben tries to knock Dominic's hat off, but Dominic ducks.

"No way. You have things to do here." I bump him with my shoulder. "Like community service at the Pidgin Beach Cat Rescue with the rest of us."

"Wonder where your old hat is," says Ella.

"Probably in Greenland by now," I say.

"You know, Greenland's ice sheets are melting at an alarming rate," Ben says. "The glaciers are shifting and dissolving and contributing to the overall global rise in sea level."

"Did you hear that, girls?" says Dominic. "Now, that's a fact for you."

I look at the two of them, and it makes me smile. I never in a million years guessed they would become such good friends. It's kind of like me and Mariella Philpotts.

Ella grabs Ben's arm and squeezes, and he puts her in an affectionate headlock. They wander on ahead of us.

Dominic bumps me back and says, "Are you glad I'm not leaving?"

I nod and smile, even though I'm getting a big embarrassment lump in my throat.

He puts his hand on my arm and I lag, then he lags. Turning around slowly, he adjusts his hat. His lips are sealed.

"What's up with you?" I ask.

His neck is turning red like he's blushing. He grabs my shoulder, almost stumbling in the process. At first, it feels like he's steadying himself, but his head is zooming toward mine, and I realize he's going to kiss me. And with the angle he's using for his approach, he's going to miss.

I try to get my lips in line with his lips, but he moves to the side. I'm thinking this is going to be a disaster. Then he parts his lips and plastic fangs appear. He's attempting to fake-bite me on the neck!

I get a mushy pretend nip before Dominic stands up, pops his fangs out, and jams them into his pocket. It's not technically a first kiss, but I'll count it as one. I lean against him to get my balance. His eyes are blinking like he's recovering from it too.

My instinct is to reach up and give him a peck on the check, but I don't.

There's the whole summer ahead for that.

* * *

By the time we get to Gusty's, Ella and Ben have already arrived, but our regular table is full up. The place is crowded with summer people, drawn in by the new sign in the window that says, *Now serving Italian coffees*. Steam billows from behind the counter, and Clooney Wickham is tapping out grounds and flipping levers like an experienced barista.

I don't mind so much that our table has been occupied, once I realize the seats belong to Edgar, Ceil, Sister Ethel, and Sister Rosie. Ceil is cradling a "double e" in her good hand and watching over Edgar's shoulder as he writes a check. His pupils seem to loop along with the zeros he pens on the small line.

Sister Ethel sits next to Ceil, her veil draped over her arm and spilling onto Ceil's wrist. She's watching the zeros just as closely as Edgar.

Ella, the guys, and I pull chairs up to the table as Edgar puts the final zero on the check, rips it out of the book, and hands it over.

Sister Ethel takes the authors' donation into her outstretched hands. "Thank you so very, very much for this generous contribution to the Pidgin Beach Cat Rescue. We can do so much with it. The archdiocese thanks you, and God thanks you too."

"And all the kitties thank you," says Sister Rosie.

"You are very welcome, Sisters—"

"And the coyote mama and the pups thank you too." Sister Rosie is not going to forget anyone.

"The pups!" Ella coos.

"They play with the cats *so* well," Sister Rosie says.

"What about the mama?" I say. "I mean, is she allowed by the cats? Didn't she . . . ?" I don't want to finish saying it, but really, I mean . . . *Esmeralda!*

"The mama is sequestered," Sister Ethel says firmly. "She is not allowed by the cats, despite the short memory of a *certain someone* who thinks all God's creatures can get along."

Sister Rosie leans back in her chair, and her face falls. "I haven't forgotten, Ethel," she says. "It's all so . . . complicated. I just can't stop myself. I have to help."

I pat Sister Rosie's arm. "I know how you feel."

## Acknowledgments

Thanks to my entire family, and especially to Chuck Hanebuth and Magda Surrisi, who support me in every possible way, and to Ellie and Michael, who have been waiting eagerly for this next Quinine Boyd book. To the entire VCFA tribe and especially the Magic Ifs and Magic Sevens. To the SCBWI gang. To all my dearest writing buddies in Hawaii, North Carolina, and around the world—you know who you are. To our new Asheville family, including Cindy and Cosby Morgan, who hosted us at the Cane Creek cottage where I wrote this book; the Harts who embody everything wonderful and welcoming about Asheville (especially my willing beta-reader, Will Hart); the Bakers, who hugged-us-up; the Walls, who were pilgrims like us and became instant and true friends; and the Weiners, who are kindred spirits in airplanes, books, and life.

Thanks to all the great people at Lerner, who make beautiful books, and especially my incomparable editor, Greg Hunter, who has perfect instincts. And my agent, Linda Pratt—I am honored to be your friend and client. And to Elizabeth Baddeley, for putting perfect faces on a couple of preternatural characters.

About the Author

C. M. Surrisi lives in Asheville, North Carolina, with her husband Chuck, two rascal Cavalier King Charles Spaniels named Sunny and Milo, and Harry, the Prince of Cats. She is a graduate of the Vermont College of Fine Arts MFA program in Writing for Children and Young Adults.